"Get back inside!"

Madelaine, blinking against the wind, raised her eyes and saw a faintly lit face, outlined ████ by her single oil lamp. It was the █████ █████ ████ █████ alcony.

"Madelaine! ██ ██ ███ ████ █████ █████ nside!" In one motion, ████ ████ ██ ████ ████ ██ waist and pulled her █ ████ ████ ████ ████ ██ her to stand away, out █ ████ ████ ████ ████ flying bits of the wind-████ ███ ████ were rushing in the window. "Stay there!" he shouted at her above the roar, and turned away.

Startled, Madelaine lunged to grab at his sleeve, pulling him back toward her. "Is Celia all right?"

The man nodded and leaned close to answer over the shrieking of the wind. "Her husband is home, and their baby and all the mares are safe." Madelaine could only stare at him, grateful, blinking her stinging eyes. Then, inexplicably, he bent and kissed her, a quick, fierce kiss that was over the instant it began. "My name," he told her, speaking so close to her ear that his lips brushed her skin, "is Françoise Jarousseau."

Look for these historical romance titles
from Archway Paperbacks.

LOUISIANA HURRICANE
1860

KATHLEEN DUEY

AN ARCHWAY PAPERBACK
Published by POCKET BOOKS
New York London Toronto Sydney Singapore

This book is a work of fiction. Names, characters, places and incidents are products of the author's imagination or are used fictitiously. Any resemblance to actual events or locales or persons, living or dead, is entirely coincidental.

AN ARCHWAY PAPERBACK *Original*

An Archway Paperback published by
POCKET BOOKS, a division of Simon & Schuster Inc.
1230 Avenue of the Americas, New York, NY 10020

ISBN: 0-671-03926-1

First Archway Paperback printing July 2000

10 9 8 7 6 5 4 3 2 1

AN ARCHWAY PAPERBACK and colophon are registered trademarks of Simon & Schuster Inc.

Cover art by C. Michael Dudash

Printed in the U.S.A.

IL 7+

For Mary Barnes,
employer, computer wizard, partner,
and most of all, valued friend.

1

Madelaine LeBlanc stood looking out the windows at the sparkling gas lamps of Baton Rouge. "It won't help to be afraid," she whispered to herself. "And no one knows what will happen."

As the music swelled to a crescendo behind her, Madelaine took a deep breath and forced herself to push aside thoughts of war. She tried to cheer herself with pleasant thoughts. This trip had been lovely. Papa's summer trips were always fun. The long ride to Baton Rouge from the homeplace on the *Belle Creole* had been a delight, with the steamboat captain as charming as any host. The packet was a beautiful paddle wheeler, with well-appointed staterooms, the beds narrow but soft. The saloon and ladies' social room had been carpeted in deep red, with chandeliers sparkling like those of any manor ballroom. The women all had dressed to the height of fashion. And Madelaine had found it easy to slip away to stand at the rail, watching the scenery glide past in daylight or the stars sparkle overhead at night. The stars had been beautiful, and she had wished ten times that Celia could have come this year. But, of course, with her new baby, she'd had to stay at home.

The city of Baton Rouge was wonderful, as it always was on these once-a-year trips when Papa mixed pleasure with his business calls on bankers and shipping-line magnates. The society here could hardly be outdone. They had attended theatricals, an opera, and a picnic ending with a horse race meeting she would remember forever for the extravagant hats the women all wore. A flock of a thousand ostriches could have no more plumes among them than had graced the hats, and certainly no plume on its original owner could be as brightly dyed!

This evening's ball was as nice as everything else had been. Judge Hector's home was beyond reproach, his wife and daughters gracious and pretty. A silent procession of house servants continually brought more food and drink.

The music ebbed and fell still, and laughter came from the dancers as they whirled more slowly, then stopped. Madelaine turned back to look at them. The warm light of the elaborate brass gaseliers danced in the polished metalwork that ran along the rim of the ceiling. They burned beautifully, merrily. Madelaine was about to turn back to the quiet vista of city lights when she saw her mother working her way free from the edge of the crowd of dancers.

"There you are!"

Madelaine smiled. Maman was tall and still slender,

and very handsome in her dramatic emerald silk gown with its cream-colored collar and cuffs of velvet appliqué. Papa had complained about the expense of shipping gowns from France at first, but Madelaine knew he enjoyed the attention it brought Maman as much as Maman did.

"Are you ill?" Madelaine's mother asked, her cheeks flushed from dancing.

Madelaine shook her head. "I feel perfectly fine."

"Then whyever would you stand off to the edge like this? When I was your age . . ."

"I know, Maman," Madelaine said, keeping her voice soft and ladylike. Indeed it was true. She knew all about her mother's youth, what a flurry of parties and hunts and balls she had graced before meeting Papa and falling in love. As a little girl, Maman had even gone to Cajun *fais do-do* and danced on cypress-planked floors from dusk until dawn with her maternal uncles and aunts and cousins. And Maman still loved dancing. She was graceful and stately at the slow Prince Imperial and sprightly as a girl when the music turned to fast songs for the galops and Deux Temps. Maman had no idea what it meant to be shy.

"Now you just stop moping, Madelaine!" Maman scolded gently. "In four short days, we will be going back home. No one on the bayou is going to entertain as much as usual this season. Your father believes everyone will become more uneasy about riding the roads as time goes on, not less."

Madelaine nodded and took a deep breath. "Maman, I—"

"No excuses, darlin' girl," Maman interrupted. "If war does come, all this will change. Perhaps forever." She swept her hand over the milling guests dressed in silk and bombazine and fine starched lace. Her eyes held a sadness so profound that Madelaine felt a chill of fear.

"Do you think there will be a war, then?" Madelaine whispered, but the moment was past. Her mother only smiled.

"You ought to be thinking of fun at your age, not politics. Leave it to the menfolk!" Maman laughed, and Madelaine felt her stomach tighten. It had been like this all her life. If anything that meant anything was ever brought up around her, the subject was changed quickly to parlor games or some elaborate skit or her piano lessons—all the things that meant nothing at all.

"Two more minutes to collect yourself," Maman said. "Then join the dancers. You are the prettiest girl here, and people wonder why you are standing apart and gazing out the windows. Two minutes, Madelaine!"

Madelaine nodded dutifully, then watched her mother walk away. It wasn't that she wanted to be serious-minded and shy. In fact, she longed to be gay and carefree like Julia and Metta, the two lovely Hector sisters who were helping their mother host this summer party—but she simply was not. She enjoyed parties, but they seemed empty, too, monotonous in an odd way. The whole spring had been a parade of picnics and horse race meetings at home. She had been in two plays, a tableau on St. Valentine's

Day that she and the Simpson girls had worked on for weeks. *And for what?* she wondered. *What good does any of it do? What does any of it mean compared to the war everyone thinks is coming?*

Madelaine took a deep breath and looked back out the window, this time seeing not the lights of the city but her own reflection. Hope, her mother's maid, had done her hair, and Madelaine had to admit that though she would always prefer Celia's touch, it did look nice. The front was frizzed perfectly, and the little beaded headdress of black velvet ribbon and gold braid set it off well enough. Her dress was a pretty flowered merino. Black silk ruchings graced the double hemline, and the waist had lace-covered Elizabethan sleeves. Madelaine smiled at her reflection, then frowned when she heard the music starting again. Deep in her heart, she knew very well why she was uneasy and bored with dancing, why everything seemed trivial to her lately.

She was terrified there would be a war and that her brothers and father would end up fighting in it. But every time she wanted to talk about it, her father shushed her. He told her to practice her French or her Italian or her piano playing or her elocution—and not to worry.

Madelaine turned back toward the dancers, knowing Maman would come get her if she didn't join in. The swirl of colored gowns looked ethereal, dreamlike, as though a good wind would scatter them like flower petals in a storm.

* * *

The shed smelled of cut grass and warm milk. Françoise Jarousseau patted old Marie's side. Her coat was rough, and he resolved to add a little lard to her grain. He loved this dear old cow. She was lop-eared and silly and looked like the devil, but she gave a full pail of milk every morning and another three-quarters at night, and she had done so for the four years he had owned her. She dropped her calves easily and regularly, and they grew up straight and fine. And beyond that, she was kindhearted and listened to him sing and whistle as though she enjoyed it. Françoise was proud of Marie. No one else had seen her value that day at the stock sale. If he hadn't bought her, the cattleman said, she'd have gone to butcher.

"I will see you this evening," Françoise told her, standing up and stretching before he picked up the pail of steaming milk. He set it high on the wall shelf, then loosened the tie rope and slid the loop over Marie's head. She turned around without further prompting and went out the shed door. She lowed once to let her pasture companions know she was coming, then hurried along, her swaying gait surprisingly fast. Françoise saw his mules and the steer he was fattening for next year's meat look up from their grazing to greet old Marie. Even they liked her.

Françoise smiled. The pigs were fed, the milking was done, and there was enough grass in the lower pasture still for all the stock. He had repaired the chicken coop to keep out the fox he had seen skulking around his barnyard. With all that done, he could gather moss today and fish on the way back, trolling a line behind his bateau.

Françoise headed back up the path, threading his way through the live oaks that stood in a thick copse behind the barn. Coming out of their long shadows, he stopped to look at the sun rising in the east. It glittered on the bayou, changing the brown water to gold.

Inside his cabin, Françoise strained the milk through a soft piece of clean muslin, then put it in the cooling basin until Antoine came. Humming to himself, Françoise washed his face and neck in the washbasin. Throwing the water out the window, he aimed for the indigo patch. It still seeded itself, even though he hadn't really taken care of it since his mother had died. He never wove cloth now. Both his sisters-in-law were wonderful weavers. He gave them milk and his extra eggs and pecans. His peach trees were among the best on the bayou, so he shared that fruit as well. He was pretty sure he would never have to weave cloth or sew clothes for himself again.

Françoise exhaled, thinking about Antoine and Pierre. His two older brothers had found women they loved. Both had children laughing and running through their houses. They were happy men. So there was hope for him.

Françoise began to whistle again as he went about his housework, a high, flutelike sound. He carried wood inside from the pile of freshly split logs behind the house. He had worked like a fool on wood splitting for nearly a month. The blisters on his palms were healing, and he had enough to last until Christmas if he was careful.

Finished with the wood, Françoise thought about making another pot of strong coffee, then decided against it. He wanted to get out on the bayou, pole upstream a ways, and find a good area for moss gathering. He hoped to find enough to help Pierre build his new room and have enough left over to sell to one of the plantations down on Bayou Lafouche. Never before in his life had he cared at all about making money, but he needed it in the worst way now.

"You are lonely," he said aloud to the ceiling. When it was kind enough not to answer, he addressed it again. "I may never find anyone with my mother's beauty and wit, I know."

"Are you awake?"

Françoise jumped at Antoine's shout from the dock. Grateful that his brother hadn't been close enough to hear his conversation with the ceiling, Françoise laughed aloud when Antoine opened the door and came in grinning. Antoine was tall, handsome, and nearly as dark-skinned as their mother had been. Françoise missed her most when he looked at Antoine—or looked into his mirror. They both had her dark skin and her blue eyes. Pierre and Jean were both lighter-skinned, both stockier, heavy through the shoulders, as Papa had been.

"You all right?" Antoine laughed. "You look startled."

"You look like Maman," Françoise said quietly.

Antoine's grin faded. "Have you noticed my oldest girl lately?"

Françoise smiled. "She will be a beauty like Maman."

Antoine grinned. "You will help me chase off the boys?"

Françoise nodded. "And Pierre, It will take all three of us and more besides." They both laughed, and Françoise slapped his brother on the shoulder, wishing they could be boys again. He imagined it: Maman and Papa cooking together in the kitchen, laughing and flirting, the summer heat heavy on the bayou, himself little again, joyous and content with no deep sorrows lodged in his heart.

2

Madelaine woke to the sound of a rising wind, and it took her a moment to realize she was home. They had slept so many places on their month-long trip that she had become accustomed to waking in unfamiliar rooms.

The storm shutters were rattling frantically in the humid, stifling darkness. Flushed from sleep, brushing her damp hair back from her face, she got up and padded barefoot across the thick carpet to her armoire. She pulled the heavy doors open wide and found her housecoat, recognizing the silvery-green silk with her fingertips.

She could barely hear the milch cows bawling in their paddocks behind the stables. The wind was high enough to have already damaged the corn and the last of the beans. At least the peas were in and shelled and safe in the cellars behind the sugarhouse. Maman had entered the weights into the ledgers the day before.

Madelaine wondered if her father was downstairs pacing as he often did in a storm. She longed to go join him, to be doing something instead of nothing. But she knew exactly what would happen if she went downstairs. Papa would shoo her back to bed, telling her he would take care of whatever came up. And he would.

"Mistress?"

Madelaine turned, looking toward the door in the darkness. "Celia?"

"Mistress? May I come in?"

"Of course, Celia," Madelaine said, but her voice was lost in a crashing roll of thunder that passed through the house, making the polished wood floor tremble beneath her bare feet. Madelaine frowned. Celia was terrified of storms. But why was she still in the house when she should be out in the quarter in her own snug cabin? Usually, she left the homeplace early to cook for her husband and care for her baby.

"Mistress Madelaine?" It was a desperate whisper.

"Celia, do come in," Madelaine said more loudly. A distant flash of lightning sifted through the slats of the closed storm battens, and Madelaine heard a familiar sound of dismay as Celia opened the door an inch.

"Mistress Madelaine," Celia whispered hoarsely. "Can I just please sit with you a while?"

"Of course." Madelaine saw a warm flicker of candlelight as the door opened another few inches. Celia's face was lit from below by the yellowish light, her fingers wound tightly around the silver candle holder. She looked ashen, scared.

"Will the cabins hold up?" she whispered.

"Of course they will," Madelaine said firmly. "They have stood since long before Papa was born." She tried to think of something else to say that would comfort Celia, but she couldn't. Things had changed in this past year. Celia was a married woman now, with a baby. Her little Daniel was asleep out in the cabins with his father. Gabriel and their son would be safe out there, Madelaine was sure, but she understood Celia's worry. The wind was coming harder and harder.

"Whyever are you in so late?" Madelaine asked.

Celia ducked her head. "Your mother had me polishin' woodwork, and it took so long! It started to lightning, and I have been waitin' for it to stop ever since, but . . ."

Madelaine gestured toward her bed. Celia had always stolen into her room during storms, from back when they had been babies. Madelaine's earliest memory was from her third year. It had been a vivid day, bright, with the soft spring air scented like magnolia blossoms. She could still see the ruffles of her starched white dress as she sat, spraddle-legged, next to Celia on the wide-planked galerie that ran along three sides of Belle Grove. They had been playing with Maman's old ribbons.

Lightning flashed. Madelaine crossed the room and took Celia's hand. "Calm down now," she said against Celia's cheek, hugging her. "Everything will be just fine."

Madelaine believed it with all her heart. Belle Grove was made of cypress beams and heavy timbers as well as brick and stone. Its columns had stood white and proud for nearly sixty years. She pulled in a long breath. The cabins in the quarters were strongly built, too, and the sugarhouse was built to stand a century, Papa always said.

"Everything is going to be just fine," Madelaine repeated, reassuring herself as well as Celia. "We haven't had a real scare in a long time." She stepped back, trying to remember the last hurricane that hit Belle Grove close enough to send Papa out into the storm, gathering up the slaves and the overseers, sending them all in every direction to check the stock, then getting everyone down to the sugarhouse to wait out the storm. She had been six, so Celia had been five and a half.

"Eleven years ago," Celia said aloud. " 'Member? They let us take our dollies."

"Come sit down," Madelaine said aloud. Lightning crackled overhead, and thunder crashed only a second or two after the light faded. It was getting closer. Celia shuddered. Madelaine almost smiled, turning quickly so Celia wouldn't see it and be hurt. This was all just so familiar. This stormy night was like a thousand other nights in their lives, Celia slipping in to sit with her.

But, Madelaine reminded herself, they were both grown now. Celia's husband was out in the cabins, sleeping on a warm bed of corn shucks and rice straw with their little son. "Come on," she said, patting the feather mattress. Celia's face lit with relief in the flicker of the candle. Madelaine smiled back, and

Celia's eyes sparkled. For a moment, it was as if they were both little girls, giggling and squealing and daring each other to run barefoot down the road before Maman caught them at such unladylike games.

"Lightnin' and thunder scares me so," Celia said, taking her place on the foot of the bed. With the next flash of blue-white, her eyes went wide, and Madelaine saw her lips move. She was scared enough to pray. The wind gusted, buffeting the shutters. Celia shivered. Madelaine took off her robe and got beneath her cotton quilt again. "Pull that extra coverlet up over yourself, Celia."

"I had bes' not," Celia said, her soft voice barely audible above the sound of the wind. "Your *maman* would have a tizzy fit if she came in and—"

"Maman stays in bed or down in the kitchen when it's storming, you know that as well as I do," Madelaine scolded.

"Yes, Mistress Madelaine. I do know that, I jus'—" Another flash of lightning stopped her voice. As the thunder rolled in the distance, Madelaine felt the bed sink a little and heard a rustling as Celia got comfortable.

Lightning brightened the room from dark to dusk, then let it go black again. Celia glanced at her in that instant, a look of gratitude and love on her face. Madelaine smiled in quick response as thunder growled in the distance. The air thickened, and Madelaine smelled the scent of rain. If it was a hurricane, it might be hours before the wind changed direction and the storm finally passed. She stared at the candle flame across the room. Between flashes of lightning, the orange glow sparkled along the bevel of the mirror's edge. She could still feel Celia trembling and reached toward her, patting the smooth cotton quilt until she found Celia's hand. As they had done since they were toddlers, the two drew closer together until they were side-by-side in the dark, holding hands, listening to the wind.

Françoise Jarousseau lay awake on his bed, arms folded behind his head. The storm was rising, but that was not what kept him from sleep. His house was built solid, the work of his grandfather's strong hands. It had stood through storms that had toppled fifty-year-old trees, and it would stand through this one.

Sitting up, rustling the Spanish moss that filled his mattress, Françoise swung his feet to the cool planked floor. This felt like a big storm, though so far, if it was, it was passing to the south. That's where most of the lightning was striking, he was sure. *Well*, he thought, smiling in the dark, *there is one good thing about a stormy night. The nightriders will stay at home where they belong.* Maybe some brave Negro men could sneak in an extra visit to their wives. Françoise bit his lip. Of all the ugly parts of a slave's life, that had to be one of the worst. To fall in love and marry, then be forbidden to live together because the wife was owned by another plantation!

Uneasy from his thoughts, Françoise stood up and stretched. He bent over the hearth and blew away the feathery ashes to reveal a glowing coal, then pulled a strand of dried palmetto from the tin beside the hearth. Blowing on the coal, touching the end of the palmetto lightly to it, he rose a few seconds later with a flame to relight his little oil lamp.

Françoise lowered the chimney glass, arching back to keep the sharp smell of the lamp oil out of his nose, then turned in a slow circle, taking in the whole *garconiere*. He loved it up here—this room he had slept in with his brothers all the while they had been growing up. But now, sometimes, it felt lonely. Antoine and Pierre had their wives and families now. And Jean had gone to sea. There had been no word from him in two long years.

"I want a wife," Françoise said to the planked ceiling. "One not unlike my mother—some beautiful woman who is much too good for me but who loves me anyway."

There was a flash of white-blue lightning that glazed the room in frosty brilliance, then flickered out. A few seconds later, thunder clashed. Françoise whistled one of his mother's tunes, the notes running as gracefully as swamp deer. Lightning lit the room a second time, and the thunder cracked close enough to make the ground shake.

"I apologize," Françoise said to the ceiling. "I did not mean to bother the heavens during such a magnificent storm." He grinned at his own joke as lightning flashed again and caught sight of himself in the little mirror on the far wall. His dark hair was falling over his forehead, and his teeth looked as white as oyster shell against his sun-dark skin. His eyes looked haunted, unhappy. Then the light winked out, and he looked dim and vague again in the yellowish glow of the lantern. The difference in the two versions of his own face disturbed him, and he looked away.

Celia woke with a start. It was still dark out, but she could hear the roosters starting to crow out in the coop behind the quarters. Through the tiny cracks in the battened shutters, she could see that the sky was graying, and she knew that the worst of the storm had passed. The thunder had rumbled on to the north by midnight, and the wind had changed direction, then dropped considerably. Celia unwrapped the coverlet from around her and eased toward the edge of the bed, careful not to waken Mistress Madelaine. She looked like a child still, in her sleep, roses blooming in her cheeks, her soft hair fanned out over the pillow.

Celia tiptoed out of the bedroom, slipping down the hall, then down the wide carpeted staircase, silent as a mouse. The cool plaster wall was beaded with water, and she kept to the outside of the stairs so she wouldn't get wet.

Lily was just coming in the side door of the kitchen, her apron already on. She wiped rain from her face with a tea towel, then laid it on the flour bin by the hall door. " 'Mornin'. You in here all night, child?"

Celia nodded. Lily was new to Belle Grove. She was a good cook, and everyone liked her well enough so far, but she was so sad it hurt Celia's heart to be around her much. Poor Lily. She was grieving her husband and children terribly. They had been sold upriver when their master died; Lily had been sold south.

"You look upset. Everything all right?" Lily asked.

"I hate lightnin' and couldn't sleep much," Celia confided. "I'm jus' now on my way out to feed my baby." Lily's face went rigid, and Celia would have given anything to take the words out of the air and stuff them back in her mouth. She started to apologize, but Lily waved her off.

"You take joy in that baby whilst you can," she said quietly.

"Yes'm," Celia said, trying to be polite and respectful. Lily had had a terrible time, and Celia felt sorry for her. But belonging to Belle Grove and the LeBlanc family was different from what poor Lily had known. Master LeBlanc would never allow his sons to separate a family like that. It'd be in his will, she was sure. "I got to go now, ma'am," Celia said respectfully. "But I'll be back in an hour or two, no more than that. If the rain keeps up, Mistress will want me wipin' walls, I expect. They bead up in this weather." Lily nodded, stepping aside so that Celia could reach for the door handle.

Hurrying across the wide veranda and beneath the pillared arch at the top of the steps, Celia picked up her skirt as the wind snatched at the cloth. Keeping her head down and her eyes half shut against the spattering rain, she light-footed her way across the wet lawn. It was cool on her bare feet, and she pulled in deep breaths, glad to be out of the close air of the big house, glad the lightning seemed to be gone.

The grass was littered with leaves from the orchards, and she glanced toward the lines of peach trees closest to the edge of the lawn. Beyond them, up past the road to the levee, were the figs and pecans. They all looked sad and bedraggled. Celia veered around the rose gardens and the well house, then skirted the long vegetable beds that stretched in a long row in front of the quarters. The tilled soil was soft, and the mud squished up between her toes as she ran past the wind-ruined okra clutching her skirt to keep her hem out of the mud spattering up from her feet.

"There you are!"

Celia lifted her head to see Gabriel standing in the doorway of their cabin. She sprinted the last hundred feet, and he caught her around the waist, swinging her in a circle, then kissing her forehead as he set her down. She looked up at him, seeing the love and worry in his eyes.

"You too scared las' night to come on back?"

Celia nodded.

"Miss Madelaine let you stay with her?"

She nodded again, and Gabriel laughed. "As good to look at as she is, she is goin' to marry young, and then what'll you do?"

"She'll be my mistress my whole life long," Celia said, believing it, afraid to believe anything else.

"You ask Miz Lily 'bout that," Gabriel said flatly.

"You hush," Celia pleaded.

From inside the cabin came an unhappy little wail that made Celia's milk come down, an achy feeling that she was used to now. She smiled at Gabriel, loving him, eager to go hold her son. She scraped her muddy feet along the edge of the porch, swinging one, then the other, through a tuft of soft grass to wipe them.

"That child is hungry," Gabriel said. Celia lifted her face to be kissed once more.

"I will love you your whole life," he said as she stepped back. "Me, not Miss Madelaine. She's *white*, Celia."

"I know that," Celia snapped, furious with him. Did he think she was a child who didn't understand how the world worked? "But she and I have been bound up together since I can remember," she said aloud. "Her heart is gold. She ain't goin' to let no harm come to us."

Gabriel shook his head, and Celia knew he was about to argue with her, but just then the plantation bell rang out, tolling steadily in its stanchion behind the big house. They both looked toward the big house.

"There'll be work and work and work to get the cane propped up and replanted after them winds," he said in a low, unhappy voice. "We'll be at it straight through fall." He pointed, and Celia saw a group of eight or ten field hands walking slowly toward the cabins on the far side of the sheep pasture. They were muddy up to their waists. "Levee patrol," Gabriel said. "They hate that bell this morning. No sleep at all for them this past night."

"I love you," Celia said impulsively. His frown erased itself, and he gave her one of his wonderful, slightly lopsided grins. Gabriel was a handsome man, and he was kind and good, and she knew that he loved her. She knew she was lucky he lived here on Belle Grove, too, not some other plantation where she would only see him at church or on weekend passes. She knew two women who had forbidden their husbands even to try to come, the way things were now with the nightriders out so often. All the people were afraid of the vigilantes.

"See you at suppertime, or maybe before," she said, trying to remind him that they were as lucky as anyone she knew. He touched the side of her face, then went down the crooked steps, heading to the left out of long habit to avoid the rotten part of the bottom plank.

Celia watched him go, heavy-footed, his shoulders down. She knew he was right. There would be long days of work for everyone to get Belle Grove back to where it ought to be. She shook one fist at the sky as she turned to go inside to Daniel. There was no earthly use for storms as bad as this one had been. None at all.

3

"All the way down to New Orleans," the marchand was saying, leaning on a dock rail. "Everything you can imagine is knocked over, torn apart." He made a groaning sound and swept one hand through the air before him. "And rain as though heaven wanted to drown us all. I almost lost my merchandise."

Françoise was spellbound, listening, glad he had come outside this dawn to drink his coffee. If he hadn't, the marchand would have slipped past unnoticed on the bayou on his way to the bigger places closer to Bayou Lafouche. The storm the week before had seemed bad enough here that it was likely even worse elsewhere. Apparently, it had been a real hurricane farther south.

The marchand gratefully sipped the cup of coffee that Françoise had fetched. "The river came up three feet, I was told. One old man told me he watched a crevasse open up in his levee, and the water just came pouring in and took his house."

Françoise squinted up at the sun, then back at the weathered face of the marchand. "It was a hurricane, then."

"A hurricane," the marchand agreed sadly. "Oaks as big around as three men joining hands. Just laid down like straw. And a murderous rain for three whole days." The marchand ran his hand through thinning hair. "Over in the Plaquemines, the rice fields are under salt water. Those folks will be years digging out of the ruins of their farms."

"We got rain and bad wind, nothing like that, though," Françoise said quietly, pitying the men with wrecked homes.

"For the first time in two years, folks have something to talk about besides secession," the marchand said with a wry laugh. "All the unionists are having to help their neighbors, no matter how they feel about them, even that old secessionist A. Franklin Pugh."

Françoise recognized the name of the powerful planter, but he didn't know the man, so he only nodded. This war everyone seemed so sure was coming worried him. The Cajuns would be better off than most, though, he was pretty sure. The swamp would keep armies out, and he had little need to leave it.

"*Bonjour!* Françoise!"

Françoise looked up the bayou and saw a bateau coming across the slow-moving brown water. The marchand followed his gaze. "My brothers," he explained. "And my neighbor Philippe. They will want to hear the news. Everyone will."

The marchand nodded, and Françoise could see that he was pleased to be the one with news. They stood side-by-side on the little dock, watching the bateau come closer. Françoise caught the mooring rope and tied up while Pierre and Antoine clambered onto his dock. "My wife says if you will stay the night and tell us all the news, she will make a gumbo you will remember for a year," Antoine said without preamble.

"And mine wants to buy thread and needles," Pierre put in.

The marchand laughed. "You have a fiddle player? And some boudin?"

Philippe smiled in his sharp, quick way. "I play a fair tune."

Antoine and Pierre laughed aloud, and Françoise joined them. It was easy to laugh on a sunny morning a week after the terrible wind and rain. He had a ruined corn crop, and his pecan trees were tattered. But his brothers and neighbors were all right. His levee had held against the waters that had risen only a little. The land below it, where his house stood sound and safe, was dry. Françoise said a silent prayer for all the people who had been truly hurt by the storm.

"It was worse down on the Lafouché," the marchand was saying. "Tore up the cane crop."

"The planters will have to sell off a racehorse or two, perhaps," Philippe said sarcastically, and Françoise laughed with the others.

* * *

Madelaine stood in the hallway, watching her father through his half-open office door. Maman had sent her to see if Papa wanted coffee, but he was talking to himself, his voice so tight and so angry that she was afraid to call his name.

"I don't have time for any of this," he muttered. He smacked his palm on the desk, and the stacks of papers quivered. Maman appeared from the dining room with Evie close behind her. Hope looked out of the parlor, too, her dust cloth dangling from one upraised hand, her reserved expression no different from usual. Maman was pale, her eyes darting from one servant's carefully blank face to another. Madelaine knew she was embarrassed at Papa's outburst.

The clacking of the knocker on the front door stilled Papa's voice, and he stood swiftly, smoothing his waistcoat as he rose. Hope rushed forward to answer it. Madelaine turned and ducked into the parlor with Maman close at her heels. Evie had gotten back inside the room first and was now polishing the brass gas fittings, pretending not to have noticed anything at all.

The front door creaked, the carved oak still swollen from the driven rain that had blown in beneath the wide gallery. "Mr. Dracil, please come in," Papa said in a cordial, calm voice. Madelaine exchanged a look with her mother. The overseer was here, which meant that Papa had sent for him. Mr. Dracil would never come to the door unannounced.

"Step into my office, if you will, sir," Papa said evenly.

Madelaine could imagine her father's face, composed, not a trace of his anger showing. He did not believe in shouting at employees, servants, or slaves— or his wife or his children. But you could always see when he was furious. He could not keep it out of his eyes.

Madelaine felt a stab of loneliness. If her brothers had been home, they would help Papa. "Maybe the boys should come home for a few months to help," she whispered, and Maman's eyes widened as she shook her head.

"*Non.* If Luc comes home, he will never go back to Paris."

Madelaine knew her mother was right. Alain had been eager to go and rarely wrote. He loved Paris and the life at the university. Luc was homesick. He would have happily lived out his life at Belle Grove. Madelaine missed him so much. Selfishly, she wished he would return home. Life was far colder without him, far more lonely. Luc would talk to her about the war, she was sure of it. And he would tell her anything he knew, too, without hiding things the way Papa always did.

The trouble was, Papa wanted Luc to be a lawyer and Alain to study the sciences, so neither would be home for a long time. Papa said it often: he wanted the LeBlancs to be known as educated and cultured—well regarded along the Lafouche and in all of Louisiana.

Papa made a sharp sound of impatience, then Madelaine heard him clearly, his voice low and angry. "I will not allow it here. Not at Belle Grove."

Madelaine leaned forward and peeked down the hall. Maman touched her sleeve, her fingers tugging at the heavy blue bombazine. She pointed toward the indoor kitchen and tipped her head in a gesture of invitation. Madelaine followed her mother down the hall, their dresses trailing along the polished floor.

"I don't know what this is about," Maman said as they rounded the corner. Lily was cutting corn from the cobs, filling a pickle crock. She looked up, then back down very quickly when she realized that Maman had not been addressing her.

"But everything is going to be all right, isn't it?" Madelaine asked. She heard the tremor in her own voice and was embarrassed. She felt frightened too much lately. When she wasn't worrying about the war, it was something else that scared her. She just felt so *helpless*—and so useless.

"Of course, *petite*," Maman said slowly. "We may have a difficult year or two, that's all."

"Is the cane all ruined?" Madelaine asked, controlling her voice this time. If she wanted to find out anything important, she could hardly sound like a terrified child when she asked.

"No, no," Maman answered. "Only some, I think. In the lowest fields, where the swamps flooded into the rows. Closer to the levees, the crop is all right, only wind-tattered."

"Here me clearly, sir. I will not have cruelty on my place." Papa's voice came down the hall suddenly.

Mr. Dracil murmured something in response, and Madelaine heard the door creaking open again. She shot her mother a glance and got only arched brows in response.

The cadenced click of boot heels coming down the hall sent Madelaine to the far side of the kitchen. Maman was a half step behind. They both reached up toward the shelves just as Papa came in, feigning some errand that had sent them into the kitchen besides their need to talk.

"Whatever is the matter, Papa?" Madelaine asked when she saw his dark expression, then she pressed her lips together, knowing it was entirely improper for her to have blurted out the question.

Papa frowned. "Lily, leave us, please." He waited for the cook to go, then took a deep breath. "A whipping. Apparently, Gabriel refused to work this morning. Said he was sick."

Madelaine caught her breath. "Is he all right?"

Papa nodded. "He will be fine in a day or two from the beating—whatever the illness is, I can't know. I have dismissed Dracil, but I have no idea where to turn now. Mr. Earley and I cannot manage everything that needs doing. I can post in the New Orleans newspaper for an overseer, but I need more hands, too."

Maman stepped forward. "Evie says that Terren Point is hiring Cajuns. Her husband told her when he was here last."

Papa narrowed his eyes. "I hadn't thought of that. It might work. We need another twenty or thirty men for a few weeks. Then we'd be past the worst." He smiled. "I am blessed with a clever wife."

Maman lowered her eyelashes, and for few seconds

she looked sixteen instead of thirty-six. Papa came close to touch her cheek. "I am sorry for the difficulties," he said softly. Then he faced Madelaine. "It has dawned upon me these past few weeks that you need a husband."

Madelaine was taken so off guard that she gasped.

Papa laughed, shaking his head. "Not immediately, but soon. Luc and Alain will be gone for another few years at their studies, I think. I want a steady-handed son-in-law to call upon in times like these." He shook his head, looking out the window. Mr. Dracil was riding past, leading a horse with a pack saddle loaded with cloth bundles.

"Look at that," Papa said. "Packed up and ready to go. Mr. Earley must have told him what I would do." He leaned on the sturdy baking table. "Dracil will have a position by sundown. He's a good man, most ways." Papa glanced at Maman. "Perhaps I was foolish to let him go. No one else I know would have."

"You are known as a kind master," Maman said, and there was quiet pride in her voice.

Madelaine glanced at the back door, a terrible uneasiness flooding her heart. This was wrong. It was all wrong. She wanted to go see Celia, to hold her friend and cry with her. Madelaine lifted her heavy skirt. She would have to change into outdoor clothes and her oldest boots, or she would ruin leather and fabric with mud. Maman would never allow that kind of wastefulness.

"Swamp Cajuns," Papa was saying quietly. "I hate to have them around the place." He glanced at

Maman after he said it, and Madelaine marveled at his lack of consideration. He often seemed to forget her parents had been just that before their land had been bought up by a sugar grower and they'd moved to a *petite habitat* near Belle Grove. Maman and Papa had met at a horse race meeting. Her father had been working as a trainer.

But Maman only smiled. "I don't see a choice just now," she said. "You can send Mr. Earley out to inquire."

Papa nodded. "I will." Then he winked at Madelaine. "I will be looking out for likely young men." Madelaine nodded uncertainly and tried to smile back, but her mind was clouded with confused thoughts. Marriage? She wasn't ready for marriage. The whole world was shifting around her. Far too much was uncertain to think about marriage. Even here, even on Belle Grove, Gabriel had been whipped. Her best friend's husband had been *whipped. The Yankees up north are right about slavery*, she thought slowly. And the thought sank into her heart. *They are. No one can practice it and have a clean soul.*

Madelaine was paralyzed by her thoughts for a long moment. She stared at her father and took a breath to speak. But he was already turning away. She started after him, but Maman grasped her arm, frowning. "Your father has business to consider now," she whispered. "Why don't you go upstairs and finish pinning the bows on the undersleeve of that blue dress?" She patted Madelaine's cheek. "Then it will be ready for the picnic Saturday."

Madelaine slowly absorbed what her mother had said. "This is more important than a picnic, Maman."

Her mother reached out and touched her cheek. "Yes. A woman's marriage determines her happiness. Her worth. But where are young men met except at picnics and parties?" Maman smiled. "Go. Pin those bows on perfectly!"

Madelaine was stunned. Her mother had misunderstood completely. She tried once more to speak, and this time her mother turned away in a rustle of starch-stiffened poplin, her flounces bobbing with her quick stride as she went back down the hall, calling to Lily, then to Hope, reminding them of tasks she wanted finished before dinnertime. The cheerfulness of her tone and the calm issuance of everyday orders to the slaves was more than Madelaine could stand. She whirled to run up the stairs, her heart pounding.

Celia stood behind Gabriel, staring at the bloody red welts that crisscrossed his back.

"Go on," Gabriel said between his teeth. "Get it done with."

Celia turned woodenly to the basin-mashed leaves and gray clay Grandma Tiley had brought by. "I never heard of this," Celia said, reluctantly pushing one index finger into the poultice. "You sure that old woman knows what she's doin'?"

"You ain't never heard of it 'cause you grew up in the big house," Gabriel said, and his voice was harsh.

Celia's eyes filled with tears. He didn't understand. And it seemed he was never even going to try. "I was

Miss Madelaine's choice," Celia said defensively. "Out of that whole line of little girls, she picked me. Ha!" She leaned forward, and Gabriel turned to meet her eyes. "And I am grateful that she did, Celia added."

Gabriel winced, lifting one arm to stretch his back. "You think it makes you special, that's why you like her so much. But it don't mean what you think. The day that family needs money, we'll be sold off anywhere and everywhere."

"You haven't been here your whole life," Celia said quietly, forgiving him. She knew it was worse other places. Much worse. He just thought it would be that bad here, too.

"I jus' don't want to hear no more about how the LeBlancs are different from other whites." His voice was low and tense, and she watched him wince as he stretched again, flexing his muscles against the pain.

"They are," Celia said quietly, staring at the terrible welts.

Gabriel jerked around and faced her. "That overseer dragged out that whip and called me a liar."

"Master LeBlanc didn't know about it."

"Master LeBlanc ain't no saint, Celia. He rides with them vigilance men, them nightriders."

She shrugged stubbornly. "You said that before, but you can't be sure, Gabriel."

He lowered his voice abruptly. "You hear that talk about people running north?"

Celia pulled in a breath, her heart hammering. "From up in Virginia, maybe," she stammered. "Nobody'd stand a chance running from down here."

She glanced around. "You hush," she whispered close to his ear.

Gabriel nodded reluctantly, and Celia exhaled. The stories were terrible. Just talking about it scared her. People had been found all bloated up and dead from snakebite in the swamps. Or the bounty hunters chased them down with dogs.

"You ever think about it?" Gabriel breathed.

Celia didn't answer.

"With the vigilantes runnin' the roads at night, things can only get worse here," Gabriel added in the same nearly inaudible whisper.

"Gabriel," Celia began. "People get killed. They die trying to run north—"

He shook his head. "Just get that mess on me so this'll stop hurtin' so bad."

Celia scooped up a little of the slippery mixture and gently rubbed it on her husband's back. "Is that all right?" she asked in a normal tone of voice.

"Jus' fine," he told her, gritting his teeth. "Jus' fine."

From the crib box, Daniel began to whimper. Celia finished, then washed her hands over the basin to get the smell off before she picked him up. When she did, she held him close, breathing in the sweet scent of his baby skin and trying to still the uneasiness in her heart.

4

❦

The night was warm. Rory Quinn's mare was lathered in sweat by the time he cantered along the last stretch of road and saw the amber glow of the signal fire through the trees. He reined in, and the mare slowed, tossing her head to fight the pressure of the bit in her mouth. There were two things he admired in a horse: speed and spirit. This mare had an abundance of both. He pulled harder, and the mare gave in gradually.

"Hold up, friend!" a voice called out from somewhere in the shadows of the trees.

"I'd be happy to, sir," Rory called out without turning his head. He forced the mare to a halt, then sat his saddle easily, keeping his hands in plain sight and well away from the pistol in his belt. The watcher would assume he was armed.

Half a minute ticked past as Rory kept a tight rein on his mare, her tail twitching in irritation as she pawed at the soft ground. Rory did not once look over his shoulder. He had been warned that the riders were cautious, that they would make sure of him before they let him join them.

"Dismount!" a second voice called out. This was an older man, his voice deeper and rougher from years of pipe smoking.

Rory dropped his stirrups, freed his feet, then vaulted to the ground and stood, holding the reins just beneath the mare's jaw. Restless, suspicious of the dark woods and the mysterious voices, she danced sideways, swinging her hindquarters away from him. In the silence that stretched into a full minute, then two, Rory heard the creaky chirrups of crickets in the grass.

"That's quite a mare," the deep voice said, and there was the sound of a chuckle from a clump of brush on the opposite side of the clearing.

"Some of you must surely know me," Rory called out. "My father is Liam Quinn, owner of Oak Hill. I am his heir." There was a murmur of voices and whispers on both sides of him.

"Come in, friend, you are welcome to ride with us tonight," the older voice announced when the murmurs faded into silence. A second later, its owner showed himself, a tall man with deep-set eyes. "Jerome Gastron." He introduced himself, stepping forward to shake Rory's hand. Rory recognized him from his father's circle of horse-racing friends. Neither one mentioned it.

Rory shook another dozen hands and noted that the men mostly had their hats pulled low. "When do we ride?" he asked them when the greetings were finished.

"We have one more to wait for," Mr. Gastron told him. "Monsieur LeBlanc is always a bit late. He has farther to ride to get here."

Rory nodded, and the men drifted back toward the fire, standing just at the edge of the light where the shifting smoke would keep the mosquitoes away. Rory tied his mare out of sight of the road and heard a number of uneasy nickers in the dark trees all around him. *The horses seem more excited about the venture than their riders*, he thought wryly. He walked back and joined Mr. Gastron just beyond the heat of the fire. They fell into horse talk, and Rory smiled when he realized that Mr. Gastron might offer to buy his mare before the night was out. The men seemed congenial, relaxed. Rory knew that he would be thought rude to ask about the man they all thought worth waiting for. One thing was obvious: none of them seemed to mind waiting.

It was nearly midnight when Madelaine tiptoed into the hall for the fourth time, still furious with her parents. The evening had been spent in arguing and tears. Papa had forbidden her to go out to the slave cabins to see Celia. Maman was concerned for her daughter's delicate nerves, she said—and Papa, the tyrant, had agreed with her. Madelaine knew they loved her, but how could they be so mean-hearted? Celia must be frantic with worry and fear.

Madelaine clenched her fists and stopped, staring into the darkness. She could still see the soft easing of the dark where her parents' door stood open. That meant Maman was awake, her candle burning low, still waiting for Papa to come up. So he was still in his office, where he might hear her come down the stairs or look out his window and see her crossing the lawns.

Madelaine hesitated, hot tears rising in her eyes. Then, slowly and bitterly, she turned back to her own room again. Her hesitation and cowardice in the face of Papa's anger had let the hour get too late anyway. Celia and Gabriel were almost certainly in bed and asleep. The slaves were rationed their lamp oil and candles and were careful to use them sparingly.

Madelaine closed her heavy oak door behind herself, holding the latch handle down to silence it. Then she crossed the thick carpet and stood, crying, before her window. *The peculiar institution.* She had heard people call slavery that all her life, but only now did it strike her what an odd phrase it was. Her parents hated abolitionists. Everyone she knew thought them unrealistic and foolish at best, insane at worst. And she was afraid in her heart that that was somehow what she had become. But try as she might, she could not rid herself of the terrible vision of Gabriel being whipped. It was wrong. Deeply and fundamentally wrong.

Through her tears, Madelaine saw that the horizon was beginning to glow with moonlight. Before long, the peach trees would have their branches traced in silver. The avenue of sixty-year-old oaks that led from the levee to the front door would be most beautiful of all.

Madelaine felt her heart sink. How long had it been since she and Celia had stolen out the heavy front doors to go look at the gigantic trees laced with moonlight? Three years? Four? Would it ever happen again? Would Celia ever trust her again? Why shouldn't Celia hate her and her father and mother for letting this happen? Gabriel would.

Madelaine's eyes spilled over. She could remember a time before she had heard the word *secession*—before she had ever overheard her father arguing with his friends about whether the South should leave the Union. It had been a wonderful time of picnics and theatricals and long summer days.

"Slavery is wrong," Madelaine whispered in the darkness, and the words seemed to free something inside her heart even as they clouded her thoughts. She had never questioned slavery any more than she had questioned sunrise. It was simply there, a part of the world she'd been born into. But now . . . ? The Northerners believed it wrong enough to threaten war.

Madelaine pressed one hand against her throat as if to calm the pulse she could feel thundering there. It was as though her whole body sensed a coming storm—one that she couldn't see or hear yet but knew would be dangerous and would change the shape of her life forever.

Monsieur LeBlanc had kissed his wife and daughter good night and retired to his office. The arguments about Madelaine rushing out to the slave cabins had taken up the last of his patience for this long, unhappy day. He had worked for hours, fussing over the figures for the coming year. He knew that the hurricane had done much more damage farther south and that he should count himself lucky. But it was hard. This storm had come at a bad time.

They had lost a few calves in the low pastures, and one litter of pigs had drowned when the sty was flooded by the creek. The horses had all been brought through well enough, but two brood mares had dropped tiny dead foals in the past week.

The real damage was in the crops. The yam fields were still wet enough that he was afraid the crop would rot. Some of the corn would recover. Not all of it. Some of the downed stalks could be picked now, the ears stored in the granary and fed out to the stock before they spoiled. But much would be lost.

As he went down the lists, the slow march of bad news began to worry him. He would probably be all right even if he had to hire labor in addition to his own slaves for a while. But not for more than a year or, if he stretched every penny to the limit, two years. No more than that. Everything would depend on a grand crop in both sugar and cotton next year. And enough yams and corn and beans to feed the place through the winter without having to buy many provisions.

Monsieur LeBlanc added the last column three or four times, looking at the expenses his sons were running up in Paris. Neither was extravagant, but travel abroad was not cheap. And the sugar machinery had set him back a year before. The new grinder and crushers had increased their cane syrup yield by nearly twenty-five percent, and in the long run the machinery would pay for itself. It hadn't yet, though.

Glancing out the window, Monsieur LeBlanc was startled to see the moon rising. It was later than he had thought. He stood quickly, shrugged his shoulders to ease the cramping he always got when he had to sit and work on his books. Then he turned toward the coat rack beside the door, reaching for his jacket and hat.

The hallway was empty. His wife and daughter had gone to bed hours before. As he went out the front door, closing it carefully so that the house servants wouldn't mark the hour of his passing, he allowed himself one painful moment of worry about Madelaine. She was a beauty, and she was clever enough to make a fine plantation wife. She was used to wealth and ease, and that was what he wanted for her. He wanted her settled before this infernal secession talk became reality.

If the war was coming, and he thought it very likely, he wanted Madelaine under the protection of some solid, wealthy family. Then, no matter what happened to him—or her new husband—she would be safe and protected. He had seen the passion in her face during her absurd abolitionist argument this evening. She was no longer a girl. He needed to choose her husband soon, or some unsuitable adventurer would catch her eye.

Monsieur LeBlanc clenched his fists and released them, angry that such an important matter had escaped his notice until tonight's explosion. There was much to consider, much to decide. If his sons stayed in Europe, they would be safe from the fighting, but would it forever injure their manhood? If there were a war, would they ever be taken seriously in the South if they had not helped win it?

Striding across the wide lawns, past his wife's rose gardens, Monsieur LeBlanc turned down the orchard road and headed for the stables. To quiet his mind, he looked at everything he passed. It was a habit, decades long. The sheds needed whitewash before long. The hayricks in the milch cows' pens were not far from needing repair.

There was a glow of light coming from the wide double doors of the stable that made him frown. Inside, he followed the light of the lantern and found Henry dozing on a mound of clean hay in the barn aisle. His usual bed was in the tack room. Monsieur LeBlanc had never liked him staying in the stables overnight unless there were mares to midwife, but Henry seemed to like it better than going home to his cabin in the quarter since his wife had died. The cabin was his sons' place now.

"Henry?"

The old man started, his eyes flying open, "Yessir? I was jus' . . . I was jus' . . ."

"Sleeping," Monsieur LeBlanc finished for him. "My fear is that one night you will stir and knock over the lantern."

Henry sat straight, rubbing at his eyes, then grunted as he got to his feet. "I'd never do that, suh."

Monsieur LeBlanc nodded. Henry certainly hadn't

done it in the past twenty years, and he probably wouldn't ever. "It just worries me. Are you listening for the roan mare?"

Henry nodded. "She's close. Tonight or tomorrow night."

Monsieur LeBlanc looked over his shoulder at the dark barn aisle. "Well, I hope the foal gets her speed and the sire's coloring. Roans are not much admired even at the racetrack these past few years. I'll need the bay gelding saddled now."

Henry nodded and made his way past. He turned down the wide center aisle, his familiar, uneven walk reminding Monsieur LeBlanc that Henry was getting old. He was a fine stableman, but it was time to assign some young slave to learn his work. Henry would teach his replacement well, there was little doubt of that. Then he could live out his life down in the cabins puttering at a little gardening or some other light work.

Monsieur LeBlanc looked out at the moon as he waited for Henry to saddle his horse. If things got bad enough, the New Orleans banks would loan him money. He had kept his contacts there, and the ones in Baton Rouge, friendly and congenial. If next year's crop wasn't enough to erase this year's debt, he'd borrow. But he knew it wasn't likely to be that simple. There was no way to tell what was about to happen up north.

Every day, he read or heard something more about the Yankees. It was clear they hated the peculiar institution. There was no telling what the South would do if Lincoln was elected come fall. The hotheads in South Carolina would almost certainly secede. That would force the hand of every other Southern state. Men who got together to play cards or hunt or run their horses ended up arguing secession instead. Monsieur LeBlanc was sick of hearing about it, but he knew it could not be ignored; there was too much at stake. South and North had to face one fact: sugar could not be grown without slave labor. Nor cotton, nor tobacco. That was the thrust of Mouton's argument, and the old man was right.

From inside the stable, Monsieur LeBlanc could hear Henry murmuring comfort words to the gelding, moving slowly to calm the animal. He wished he could do the same for his neighbors and friends. Calmness was what was desperately needed now. No one could defend the right or wrong of slavery, even though Calhoun wrote endlessly on the topic. It simply *was*.

Monsieur LeBlanc ran one hand through his hair, then replaced his hat. He had not invented slavery, and he practiced it as fairly and justly as anyone he had ever met. Right or wrong was not the point. There had always been slaves, throughout the history of mankind, and sugar could not be grown without slaves. The Northerners didn't mind buying sugar, now, did they? And their free mill workers often ate less well and lived in far worse conditions than any slave. Free? Free to starve and die of cold and want? The damn Yankees were just too big for their britches, telling the rest of the world how to live.

Monsieur LeBlanc glanced at the moon. It was rising fast and was nearly full. There would be enough light to ride hard. Henry finally led the gelding toward him saddled and ready. Monsieur LeBlanc squared his shoulders and put thoughts of war aside. There were problems closer to hand.

It was time to clean up the countryside once and for all. Thieves, mendicants, and violent men would find soon that there was no place left to hide in Lafouche Parish. If decent men took action, perhaps the bayous and the prairies beyond would become the paradise their Maker had intended. Monsieur LeBlanc followed Henry and the gelding out the double doors. He hoped what he was doing was right, joining these vigilante rides. He was one of the level heads, he knew. There had been beatings that would have turned into lynchings if he hadn't been present.

Henry limped to a halt and turned the fidgeting gelding so that he could mount. Monsieur LeBlanc watched him closely, trying to remember how old Henry's sons were. He had two, or perhaps three. Maybe one of them could take over the stables. A way with horses sometimes ran in families. His own sons were better horsemen than most.

Monsieur LeBlanc heard Henry grunt as the old man gave him a leg up, and he resolved to ask about his sons. Henry would be the best judge of which should be taken from field work and set about a higher occupation.

Gabriel lay on his side in the darkness, the whip cuts on his back stinging like fire. The mud poultice had helped a little for a while, then the pain had come back full force. He listened to Celia's quiet breathing and the breathing of his son in the crib box beside their bed. But instead of soothing him, it brought a surge of fury so strong he nearly lost hold of himself.

Biting his lower lip to keep from screaming his anger, Gabriel forced himself to calm down, even as he tasted blood. Waking up everyone in the quarter would do him no good. In fact, it could do him harm. A reputation for being wild and unpredictable just got a man watched closer.

Celia stirred in her sleep, and Gabriel held very still, trying not to wake her with the anger that clawed inside his belly and chest. There was talk that Northern politicians were against slavery. Old Henry had heard a man speechify on a New Orleans street corner the last time he'd been taken along to judge the worth of auction bloodstock. Master LeBlanc had hurried everyone out of earshot.

The sound of hoofbeats caught Gabriel's ear. One rider, moving slowly to be quiet. Gabriel lifted his head. The rider was keeping to the grass on the side of the lane, too. After a few minutes, the hoofbeats began to fade. Just before the sound dissolved completely, Gabriel heard the hoofbeats quicken into a gallop. That far from the house and the quarters, the rider apparently had no further need for silence.

5

✤

Robert Sheldon approached the carved oak doors slowly. There was colored glass set in glazed panels on either side, and he saw a shadow move past it. The servants were expecting him, waiting to let him in. He took a deep breath, glancing at the splendid rose gardens, then spotting chimney stacks of the sugarhouse most of a mile away. This was a big place, a perfect place. His wife would be happy here, he was sure. Far happier than she was living on Godlier Park. She loved to help with the big soirees, the race meetings—and there would be many more here.

Sheldon straightened his coat and cleared his throat. Then he lifted the brass knocker, marveling at its weight and shine. He barely had time to release it before the door opened. A tall housemaid motioned him in upon hearing his name. He stood in the entry hall as she left, looking up. The ceilings were high and painted elaborately. And they had modern gaseliers, the long curves of gilt and brass as graceful as swans' necks. He could see the Brussels carpets in the next room, too.

"Mr. Sheldon?"

He turned and saw Monsieur LeBlanc. The man looked different in the light of day. They both nodded politely, and Sheldon could tell he had been recognized, too. Neither of them would mention the night rides, he knew. But it couldn't hurt that Monsieur LeBlanc knew they held similar politics.

"I came to apply for the position of overseer, sir," Sheldon said as though he were speaking to a complete stranger.

LeBlanc nodded. "Come into my office, please, sir." Sheldon waited for Monsieur LeBlanc to open the heavy oak door.

The morning was hot and still. There was little sound in the swamp; even the birds were dozing in the trees. But Antoine was breathing hard, and Françoise could only stare at him.

"They did what?" Françoise demanded. His stomach was tight, and he felt sweat beading on his own forehead.

"They beat him senseless," Antoine rasped. "They whipped him and told him to get out of the Lafouche Parish by this morning. He went, barely able to walk at all. His woman was paddling because he could not, in that leaky old *pirogue* of her father's." Antoine had run from the levee up to the house, barely pausing to tie his flat-bottomed bateau to the dock.

Françoise shook his head, trying to absorb the terrible news. "A week ago?"

"They always come around full moon," Antoine added. "And find someone helpless and blameless and—"

"Helpless maybe," Françoise interrupted. "But Lanille is a crooked trader—"

"Don't defend these nightriders to me, Françoise," Antoine said coldly. "Lanille is an old man."

Françoise nodded. "He is. But it was only two years ago that he was accused of shooting that gambler."

Antoine made a fist and punched at the air. "Accused by rumor and gossip, never more than that. You know why they came to his house, you just won't admit it."

Françoise looked out toward the bayou. He did know. And his brother was right, he didn't want to admit it.

Antoine made a sound of disgust. "There is little use in trying to hide from it, Françoise. They beat him because his father was mixed blood. They hate the very idea of a free man with mixed blood. Like ours," he added, and Françoise jerked around to face him, a cold knot in his stomach.

"Antoine, you don't know this for certain. Lanille has lived on the wrong side of decency his whole life. He has traded dishonestly enough that it was the same as stealing. He lies. He asks for help but rarely offers it. He's—"

"I know what he *isn't*," Antoine stopped him. "He's not *white*."

Françoise was silent a moment. He knew Antoine

was right, in a way. Louisiana was a *gumbo* of mankind. Germans married Cajuns, Irish and French were cousins; their American-born children were all called *Creole*. Many Creole families had African blood in their veins as well, but few admitted it if they didn't have to. It made no sense, but there it was. All the white races could mix, and no one cared too much. "Once the slaves are free . . ." he began, but his brother made a sharp sound of disgust.

"When pigs fly? When hell cools to ashes? And when will this happen, Françoise?"

Françoise shrugged. "Lanille offended many men for many years. Maybe he wronged one of these nightrider vigilantes."

"Say what you will," Antoine shouted. Then he dropped his voice. "Just be careful, Françoise. Stay clear of the planters and the cattlemen."

Françoise stared at his brother, suddenly understanding. "So, you are not going to Belle Grove with me tomorrow?"

Antoine leaned toward him. "More than that. I hope to dissuade you from going."

Françoise looked at the sky, then at the two oaks that grew in his yard, then at the shabby old house that stood between them. "I want to repair the house, Antoine. Make it fit for a wife."

"Then fix it a bit at a time, slowly, like Papa did. You won't need money. You have your brothers and cousins and—"

"And it will take years," Françoise said quietly. "I want brass hinges and a carpet and a new rope bed."

"You are a young man." Antoine laughed.

Françoise scowled at him. "I am hoping to find a bride, Antoine. Soon."

"And she will understand that a proud old house needs care and patience," Antoine said.

"Not all women are as patient and good as your Sophie," Françoise said, to appease his brother. And it was true. Antoine had married well.

They embraced, touching their cheeks for an instant. Antoine ruffled Françoise's hair as he had when they were boys. "Just forget about what that Mr. Earley told the marchand, eh? Stay here on the bayou where you belong."

Françoise stepped back. "I will consider what you have said to me. But I will try this plantation work for a short while."

Antoine shook his head. "Don't be stubborn, Françoise. You know what Maman used to tell us."

" 'Stubborn and proud hold hands until stubborn makes them both fall,' " Françoise recited, then pivoted to stare at the front of his house. He took in a long breath. Antoine was likely right about it being safer to stay away from the planters now. But Lanille was a dishonest man who had made a lifetime of enemies. And while mixed blood wasn't approved, the whole of Louisiana was full of people like himself. Black and white had lived too long and too close together for it to be otherwise.

"I am going," Antoine said, clapping him on the back. Françoise nodded, still staring at the house as his brother started back toward the dock.

Maman and Papa had loved each other fiercely, ignoring all the initial objections from Papa's parents to the idea of Maman's mixed blood. Parrain had come to love his mother, Françoise knew. They all had—and very quickly. She was proud and beautiful and intelligent. Papa had always claimed that his parents could never believe that such a woman had condescended to marry him.

Françoise also thought his father amazingly lucky. Papa had been a good, honest man who had tended his land and his family and had danced until dawn at every *fais do-do* that was close enough for him to go to. He had been respected. But Maman had been extraordinary, a *traiteur* who healed the sick, a fiery woman whose advice and counsel were sought. Men stayed near her like bees around flowers; women liked her for her honesty and kindness.

"A wife like Maman would be too much to ask?" Françoise said aloud, then realized that Antoine had stopped and was looking at him.

You won't marry at all if the nightriders find some reason to hate you," Antoine called.

"Why would they?" Françoise said angrily. "I'm not a criminal."

"They are not always so reasonable as that."

Françoise shrugged, and Antoine waved once more and headed back up the path. He untied his bateau and paddled away without so much as glancing back.

"Is he healing all right, then?" Madelaine asked, watching Celia iron.

Celia nodded and replaced the ruffle crimper on the hearth. She stood up, pressing her hands to her back. "Healing real fast, Mistress. He worries me, though." She pressed her lips together, knowing it was exactly the kind of thing that Gabriel would not want her to say to Mistress Madelaine.

Madelaine tipped her head. "There's too much work, I know. Papa is nearly dead with fatigue every night himself."

Celia shook her head cautiously, wishing she hadn't said anything at all. "Then what worries you?" Madelaine asked. Her eyes were steady, kind, concerned.

Celia sighed. There was no answer she could give Miss Madelaine. Gabriel worried her because he wanted his freedom bad enough to talk about running away. And that could get him killed. "I s'pose everything is really all right," she said.

"Is it anything I can help with?" Madelaine pressed, her expression intense in that odd way it had been since the whipping. "Do you need more food or blankets or—"

"No, no, nothin' like that," Celia said quickly. This was something else she couldn't explain. It always caused trouble when she came out of the big house carrying a stack of gifts from Mistress Madelaine. The other women, especially the younger ones, glared at her for days. Small gifts she could hide in her apron were better. Extra food was the best thing about working in the big house. Not even Gabriel turned his nose up at food they could eat in private.

Celia pressed her lips together again and lifted the sprinkle bottle. She dampened the fabric expertly, working her way around the ruching that trimmed the bottom tier of ruffles. She hated this gown, even though it looked beautiful on Mistress Madelaine. It took a day to undo the seams and wash it, then another full day to iron it.

"I wish you could just tell me," Madelaine whispered. "Maybe someday when you are free, we can—"

"Hush!" Celia hissed, then covered her mouth with her hand. Her heart pounded in her chest. Miss Madelaine had no idea the trouble she could bring down with talk like that. *If her maman overheard* . . . Celia forced a smile and pulled in a quick breath. "He says he's jus' real tired. Like you said about your papa."

Mistress Madelaine nodded and smiled, but she was searching Celia's face as if some treasure lay hidden there. Celia looked down at her work. Madelaine finally answered in a light voice. "Papa hired some Cajuns last week. I haven't seen any of them yet, have you?"

Celia shook her head. "No. But I know they're here."

Madelaine sighed, but Celia refused to look up when she spoke. "Mr. Sheldon told Papa some of them are going to camp up along the marsh."

Celia picked the crimper off the hearth, using the flannel hot cloth to pad her hands. She spit on the iron to test it. Her saliva hissed into nothing in an instant. A little too hot. She set the iron in its stand at the end of the ironing table and turned to face Mistress

Madelaine. "Gabriel said some camped down at the levee last night and stole a few okra."

Madelaine shook her head. "Maman is worried about that. That they will steal. Maybe I should tell her they already have."

Celia arched her brows, wishing she hadn't said it. She had no wish to bring trouble down on the Cajuns, either. "They only took a few. Maybe they didn't have enough for supper." She reached for the iron and spit again. It was perfect this time, a long hiss. She set it in the frame again, just long enough to make sure the first stretch of fabric was dampened perfectly and lying smoothly. Then she picked it up and opened its jawlike halves, sliding the ruffle in quickly, closing the crimper until the hissing inside faded. Instantly, she opened it and slid the next section of fabric in.

"You are so good at that," Madelaine said. "I tried it once and nearly put a hole in a new gown."

Celia was struck by a sudden memory. She had begun learning to iron when she was so small her chin had barely cleared the table edge. And the first time she had put a hole in something, old Bertha had whacked her hard. Her head had ached for days.

"I just don't see how you can do it without ruining the cloth," Madelaine was saying.

Celia nodded. "Takes practice. Miss Bertha taught me how."

"I miss her sometimes," Madelaine said wistfully. "She was my only aunt on my father's side, you know."

Celia said nothing. She opened the crimper and saw the slight, telltale softness in the tiny ironed-in pleats that meant the heated iron was cooling off. She lifted it and set it back on the stove. Then she picked up the flatiron and turned back to the table, starting to work on one of the huge leg o' mutton sleeves while the crimper heated.

"Do you remember how she used to get angry with us for being too noisy outside her room?" Madelaine asked suddenly.

Celia nodded. She remembered old Miss Bertha all too well. All the people did. There had been no real tears at that funeral, not on the quarter side of the gathering. The old woman had bullied, scolded, and slapped every one of them.

"Did she ever show you her false tooth?" Madelaine asked, and there was a giggle hiding in her voice. For an instant, she sounded as she had when they were little. Celia smiled.

"She surely did," she said, deftly smoothing the heavy cloth of the wide sleeve as she went, nosing the flatiron along slowly enough to take out all the wrinkles but not slowly enough to burn.

"Remember how she would point at it and then try to talk at the same time?" Miss Madelaine put her index finger in her mouth as if she were pointing at a gold molar. Then she frowned an old Bertha frown. Celia laughed a little. Mistress Madelaine had a knack for mimicry.

"Add dend," Mistress Madelaine said, imitating her dead aunt's croaking speech, "day put da gode odd top ob da wood."

Celia burst into laughter. Madelaine grinned, still

talking nonsense with one finger in her mouth. Celia set down the iron, afraid she would drop it. Madelaine laughed with her.

"Madelaine!"

The sharp voice from the hall made Madelaine hush instantly. Automatically, Celia turned and faced the hearth, reaching for her sprinkler bottle, dampening the unironed portion of the sleeve, her head bent over her work.

"Madelaine! I heard you laughing like a donkey. Where are you?"

"In here, Maman," Madelaine answered, blushing.

"Ah, Celia is here, too. I might have known," Maman said, her morning dress filling the doorway, the hoops beneath the skirt jiggling as she tapped her foot. "You two are far too silly for your age," Maman said tersely, but there was a twinkle in her eye. Celia saw it and allowed herself a deep breath. Madelaine noticed, too, because she came forward, her own wide skirt flouncing with her movements.

"I can't think what we can do with you," Maman said, pretending to stare at the ceiling as if deep in thought. "There must be something—"

"What, Maman?" Madelaine asked. "What secrets are you keeping?"

Mistress LeBlanc laughed, and Celia allowed herself to smile just a hair's breadth. Mistress was never cruel and almost always generous and fair, but she did not like the house servants acting too familiar with her or any member of her family—no matter how friendly she sometimes acted toward *them*.

Madelaine turned back toward Celia, an exaggerated

grimace on her face. "I know what it must be. Maman is going to make me take piano tutoring again this winter."

Celia made a practiced face. "You poor thing, Mistress Madelaine, I know how you hate bein' cultured and accomplished."

"Enough teasing, both of you," Maman interrupted. "Celia, you mind your work, and Madelaine, I want you to practice a ladylike smile and a soft, musical laugh before Sunday."

Madelaine frowned. "Why? Are we having special company?"

Celia glanced up. Mistress LeBlanc was shaking her head. Lifting the crimper from the hearth, Celia was only half turned when the mistress sighed so wistfully she sounded like a girl.

"On next Friday, yes, dreary bankers and their equally dreary wives. But on the following Sunday, Madelaine," she said in a low voice, "your father has invited a young man to supper. A *suitable* young man."

Celia glanced up in time to see Miss Madelaine blush. "Maman, you should not tease me like this."

"I am not teasing," Maman said. "His name is Rory Quinn. He is half-Irish, but the other half is good French stock. His is a good Catholic family and well off, and he lives only a day's ride to the southeast. And . . ." She paused for dramatic effect, and Celia watched her face become positively girlish.

"And what?" Madelaine demanded.

"Your father says he is quite an appealing young man."

Madelaine smiled tremulously, and Celia stared at

her. She was beautiful with her cheeks flushed pink and her lovely eyes open wide. Any man would fall in love with her. Her brothers' friends had all begun noticing her five years before, when she was barely twelve. With her brothers gone, though, for the past two years, there had been few young men around the place. Madelaine was going to blush and glow her way through the whole evening. Celia smiled as she ironed. This Rory was in for the surprise of his life.

"Celia?"

"Yes, ma'am?" Celia looked up and met Mistress LeBlanc's eyes as she lifted the iron from the cloth.

"After you finish this one, get the chocolate-colored velvet and moiré silk taken apart. I think it would be good to have that one clean and fresh, too, just in case we have a cool evening come next Sunday night."

Celia nodded. "Yes, ma'am."

The mistress went out, and Madelaine leaned close. "Rory! What an odd name."

"It is," Celia agreed, thinking unhappily about the yards and yards of moiré silk she would be facing that evening.

"I won't say it again," Madelaine said suddenly.

Celia made her face expressionless instantly, knowing what she meant and hoping she would let it drop. But she didn't.

"But one day when you are free, and I pray it is soon, we can really be friends. Please?"

Celia looked into Madelaine's eyes and wanted to tell her that they already were like sisters, but she knew it wasn't really true, no matter what she always told Gabriel. So she just nodded and smiled, then went back to her crimping.

Henry stepped out of the stable, blinking in the sunlight. It was hot this morning and going to get hotter by midday, that much was sure. He could hear the milch cows in their sheds on the other side of the creek that ran down the slope in back of the stables.

"Should I come with you or finish this?" Gabriel called from the doorway.

Old Henry turned abruptly. "Stay in there and get them stalls cleaned out." Gabriel nodded and turned back to his work.

Old Henry stopped alongside the fence of the yearling paddock and shook his head in disgust. This Gabriel was a field hand, and he didn't seem to have any horse sense at all. So why had Master LeBlanc seen fit to put him here?

Henry spat into the dirt. He had two fine sons, and both broke their backs in the cane every day of the world. And both of them had more of a touch with horseflesh than this man. But Gabriel's missus had been in the big house her whole life. So he was going to get special treatment because of that until the end of time. It wasn't just, but there it was.

"Do you want me to go right on to the next stall?" Gabriel shouted from the doorway.

"Of course!" Henry turned back toward the stable. Was he trying to rile him?

Gabriel disappeared inside again. Henry stared out at the yearlings for a minute more. Maybe something would happen to Gabriel. It would if he didn't learn to move more slowly around the horses. Men who moved too quick and talked too loud often got kicked. Sometimes they were killed.

"Is there drinking water up here, sir?"

Henry looked up to see a man dressed in homespun walking toward him. The thick French accent and the woven palmetto work hat gave him away instantly. This was one of the hired Cajuns. Henry straightened his spine and faced the man. "No water here for you, sir. Over by them hog pens, maybe."

The man looked startled, then he narrowed his eyes and came closer, lifting his head to let the sun strike his face. Henry saw the color of his skin and was sorry, but he could hardly take the joke back now. Then the man shrugged and walked off whistling. The sound was like a silver flute, and Henry stared after him.

6

❧

Françoise had no idea where the hog pens were, but he wasn't fool enough to try to find the stinking wallows the stableman had directed him toward. It was time to get back, anyway—dinner break was no doubt about over.

Françoise walked a little faster, looking around. It was a good farm. And things were going all right, in spite of all of Antoine's warnings. This was the fourth day he had worked at Belle Grove, and so far the work was no worse than what he was used to. He had gotten tired of paddling home in the dark and returning before daybreak, though. Antoine had reluctantly agreed to milk old Marie and feed his other stock so he could join the growing camp of men at the edge of the cane fields by the swamp.

Françoise quickened his step, setting his sights on the tall smokestacks of the sugarhouse. He was working in the field just behind it. There was water for the hands to drink—it was just warm and stale-tasting from the old buckets it was kept in. He had been hoping for something cooler and fresher.

Françoise looked at the stock as he went back past the maze of corrals and sheds behind the stables. The milch cows were some breed he didn't know. He wished he could talk to the planter about them. Past the stock, the orchards began again. He had spent a few minutes examining the shapes of the peach trees when he had come through them. But he stopped twice more this time as well. The pruning was done very differently from the way his father had taught him, and he thought it might make for a better crop, if not a stronger tree. The first limbs began too low. But above, Monsieur LeBlanc—or some knowledgeable slave—had opened up the centers of the trees, trimming them into growing like a wide-mouthed goblet, letting sunshine down into the branches to help the blooms and, later, the ripening peaches.

Françoise whistled a little, examining the places where limbs had been shortened or removed, taking in the different method, resolving to practice it on two of his own young trees, to see what he thought after a few years' growth. The big farms were strange to him. This was at least one thousand arpents, maybe more. It seemed to go as far as the eye could see.

Françoise was sorry to have offended the old stableman with his presence, and he could understand the man's reaction. Belle Grove had been invaded by wage hands doing the work he had probably had to do as a young man simply to eat and avoid the whip. Rage and resentment were in the core of every enslaved man, Françoise was sure. How could it not be?

Françoise came out of the far side of the peach orchard, noticing that there was not a single peach on the ground—though the wind from the storm had to have knocked all the late ones off. The mistress of this plantation saw to details.

At the edge of a cornfield he had skirted to the north a few minutes before, Françoise veered south, walking along the outside row. Much of the field had been laid flat. It would be hard work to go through the tangle of stalks to get the good ears picked, but there was little else that could be done.

Françoise looked to his left and saw the hog pens and smiled wryly. The creek was indeed wallowed out and full of pig dung. He picked up his pace. It hadn't seemed he had walked this far. What did it take for a man to get a place this big? Most likely, it was family money earned by being born into the right crib.

The place was well cared for, Françoise admitted. He had to respect Monsieur LeBlanc for that, at least. He had not liked the man much, with his polished black boots and his perfectly combed hair. He had an air of arrogance about him, walking up and down the line of newly hired men like a general inspecting his troops before battle.

"And you are not used to working for another man," Françoise reminded himself in a low voice. "Nor will you ever be."

Françoise began to whistle again, one of the high, silvery tunes his mother had favored. They were Irish tunes, he had been told by several people who had heard him whistle them. Françoise wished that Maman was alive to ask. Where she had learned the tunes, and from whom, was a mystery he would never be able to solve now that she was dead.

"You sound like some kind of bird," a woman's voice called out.

Françoise turned, startled. There, sitting a fine horse, was a beautiful girl. She wore a wide-brimmed riding hat but her cheeks were flushed with the heat of midday. Her skirts draped over her sidesaddle, belling outward from her tiny waist. Her hemline was spattered with mud. She had been galloping.

"Madelaine!"

This was a man's voice, and as he galloped up, Françoise recognized Monsieur LeBlanc. "Is this man addressing you?" he asked the girl.

She shook her head, her shining hair light and lovely on her shoulders. "No, Papa. I addressed him. He was whistling, and I simply—"

"Go on to the house now." Monsieur LeBlanc cut her short.

Françoise watched without breathing as she tossed her head and pulled her mount around to the left. Urging the big bay into a gallop, the girl disappeared around the wind-ravaged corn.

"Have you been sent on an errand?" Monsieur LeBlanc asked in a clipped, cold voice.

Françoise shook his head. "No, Monsieur LeBlanc. I wanted to see your peach trees and how you pruned them."

Monsieur LeBlanc's eyes narrowed slightly. "Why?"

"To compare your methods with my own," Françoise said matter-of-factly. If the man was going to discharge him for being this far from the cane fields, there was nothing he could do about it. Humbling himself would not help.

Monsieur LeBlanc's eyes narrowed into slits, then widened when Françoise calmly met his gaze as the seconds ticked past. Françoise knew that this man was used to overseers and slaves who looked aside, not matching his direct stare.

"The method seems sensible to me," Françoise said into the awkward silence.

"Does it?" Monsieur LeBlanc answered, a look of wry amusement on his face.

"All but the first scaffolding of the trunk," Françoise added, almost enjoying the conversation. He had rarely seen a man caught so off guard. Monsieur LeBlanc's face was like a boy at a circus, astounded when the parrot can talk.

"And what," Monsieur LeBlanc demanded, "is wrong with that?"

"With the scaffolds that low, the trunks are shaded," Françoise told him evenly. "Bark rot sets in easier. The shade keeps them damp."

Monsieur LeBlanc's eyebrows gathered in a frown. "We have had some trouble with the bark rot."

Françoise nodded. "I don't doubt it. Now, if you will excuse me, sir," he said, lifting his hand in salute, "I was only to leave my work for a few minutes, and I have spent them all. You have a very good farm here," he added, meaning it.

Monsieur LeBlanc stared at him again, obviously uncertain what to say to a workman who had politely sent him on his way. Especially a Cajun workman as dark-skinned as some of his slaves. Françoise frowned to keep from laughing and started off, resisting the urge to look back. After a dozen strides, his thoughts left the pompous Monsieur LeBlanc and turned back to his beautiful daughter.

Henry saddled Mistress Madelaine's bay early the next morning, as well as the big-boned sorrel gelding Master LeBlanc was favoring for field riding these days. He could sense a tension between father and daughter and studiously ignored the awkward silences between them.

As he watched them ride off, he heard faint shouts in the distance, over toward the sugarhouse. He stared in that direction as though staring hard would enable him to see through the peach trees and cornfields and pastures to the other end of the plantation. He could only hope that whatever the trouble was, it had nothing to do with his sons. Henry spit on the ground. If he could get even one of them out of the cane fields for good, he would die happy. He wanted to save both of them from the crippled-up old age of the other quadragenarian field hands on the place.

Madelaine sat her horse, watching the Negroes raking a pile of bagasse, turning it to keep it dry.

Sudden shouts made her turn. What she saw made her heart ache. One of the driver's boys, a boy no more than fourteen, had come off a wagon seat, pitched sideways by the wheel dropping suddenly into one of the unrepaired mud bogs left from the storm. He had fallen close to a pile of heavy wooden hogsheads. He was bent double, clutching his head. A group of slaves came to stand around him in a loose circle, and Madelaine could no longer see. She sat still, saying a prayer.

The sudden appearance of one of the Cajuns startled Madelaine. He came walking out of the cane field and strode toward the circle of Negroes surrounding the hurt boy. She couldn't hear what he said to them, but they stood aside to let him pass. When they moved, she watched him kneel beside the hurt boy. He stayed in that position for a long moment, and Madelaine wondered if he were praying, too.

Very slowly and deliberately, the Cajun placed his hands on the boy's shoulders and pulled him gently into a sitting position. It was then that Madelaine saw that the boy's right arm stuck out at an unnatural angle. The Cajun was asking the boy questions, Madelaine could tell, because the boy shook his head, then nodded, his whole body shaking with pain. Madelaine started to pull her gelding around, to ride for the big house to tell her mother to send for the Terre Bon doctor. It was obvious the boy's arm was broken. Then she heard a scream and turned back, horrified. The Cajun was holding the boy's arm straight up, and, as she watched, he braced himself and yanked hard. A second scream rent the air. Then the boy was sobbing.

After a moment or two, the Cajun pulled the boy slowly to his feet and touched his shoulders again, then walked behind him, circling him once, slowly, as though he were looking for any other injuries. A woman emerged from the sugarhouse, looking frantically across the yard. She ran toward the boy, shouting incoherently as she broke through the watchers and threw her arms around the boy.

The Cajun stood back, giving the mother room to weep and question her son. The boy flexed his arm, turning his palm up, then down. He smiled. The Cajun smiled back, then turned and looked across the yard.

Madelaine knew the instant he spotted her because his face lit with a grin. He tipped his straw hat and pointed at the boy, then nodded, an exaggerated motion, the smile still on his face. The boy was all right.

Madelaine felt the oddest stirring in her heart, looking at the Cajun man's face. He looked so relieved, so joyful, it was almost as though he had known the boy—though she knew that was impossible. After a few seconds, Madelaine couldn't help but smile back at him, and she lifted one hand to wave. He bowed as if bending over an invisible lady's hand and kissed the air gallantly. Madelaine laughed and pretended to withdraw her hand as gracefully as he had pretended to kiss it. Still smiling at her, he straightened and walked away, turning back to wave when the mother called a thanks after him. Madeleine watched until he disappeared into the rows of cane. Only when she could no longer see him did she hear him start to whistle.

The silvery sound was lost in the rising noise of the slaves as they suddenly hurried back to their work. Madeleine looked up and saw Mr. Earley galloping up the road. Someone had run to tell him about the accident.

She pulled her gelding in a half circle and urged him into a canter up a side road into the orchard, hoping Mr. Earley hadn't seen her. The Cajun man had done a good deed, and she did not want him sent off because he had made a flirtatious gesture her father would disapprove. Feeling oddly giddy, Madeleine galloped the roads, pulling off her hat to let the wind take her hair.

Celia came out of the big house early—because she knew she would have to go back to help Mistress Madeleine dress for the bankers from New Orleans. It made her angry. Wasn't it just like Mistress LeBlanc to decide that on top of trying to repair the storm damage to the crops and the gardens and the house—and working everyone half to death to do it—they should have a dinner party or two.

The one next Sunday would be different. Celia was looking forward to peeking in at the proceedings. Mistress Madeleine wasn't talking about it much, but when she did, Celia could tell how excited she was to meet the mysterious Mr. Quinn. But this one, the bankers and their wives, would be dull at best and would drag on half the night. Celia dreaded the boredom of waiting for the guests to leave so that she could help Mistress Madelaine undress and get her to bed.

At least, Celia thought, walking fast and swinging the cloth bundle Lily had made up for her, *Gabriel is through with field work now.* She was so grateful. Cane broke men's backs, and the snakes in the fields killed a man now and then.

Stableman was a much better position, better for Gabriel than carriage driver or anything in the big house. He wouldn't have to look down and murmur and serve wine on trays. He would never be good at that. Mistress Madelaine, bless her loving heart, had put just the right bee in her father's ear. Master LeBlanc valued his horses. It was an important job.

Celia walked up the row of cabins, nodding and smiling at people who greeted her. They knew why she was in a hurry, and none of them invited her to stop and rest or chat until she came to her favorite cabin on the whole row—Grandma Tiley's. She liked the old woman, but it was her precious Daniel she was eager to see every evening.

"He was good all the day long," Grandma Tiley said, gesturing toward the cracker box that served Daniel as a crib here. "He's growin' quick-like."

Celia nodded, setting down her cloth bundle. She reached into her pocket and pulled out the packet of cinnamon she had hidden there earlier. Grandma Tiley's face lit up, then went stern. "Why, chile, you shouldn't be takin' nuthin' from the big house."

Celia smiled. "It's all right, Grandma. They got a full hogshead in that upstairs storeroom. I asked Mistress Madelaine."

Grandma Tiley's eyes went wide as she imagined that much cinnamon. Celia patted her shoulder and went to pick up Daniel. He woke and laughed happily when he saw her face. He was growing fast. Every day, she left the big house once or twice to nurse him. And he always wanted to nurse three or four times during the night. Unbuttoning her dress, Celia sat in Grandma Tiley's only chair to feed her son while the old woman clucked and cooed over the cinnamon and the puddings she was going to make with it. Celia stood up when Daniel was full and falling asleep in her arms.

"I surely thank you," Grandma Tiley said at the door. Celia nodded and kissed her wrinkled cheek, grateful that the old woman was willing to take care of Daniel in exchange for a small gift now and then. She didn't want to leave him with Auntie Emma and Mrs. Hain. They were nice enough women, but they took care of everyone's babies; the crib boxes lined the floor of their cabin. Daniel loved being held, and Grandma Tiley sat with him, rocking and talking, all day long.

As she got home, veering to the left to miss the rotten plank in the bottom step, Celia pushed open the cabin door with her shoulder. She laid down her bundle of leftover pork pie on the table, then settled Daniel in his crib box. Then she turned to the washbasin. Gabriel didn't like the perfume that clung to her hands after she did Mistress Madelaine's hair. She washed up to her elbows, then dried herself on a flannel cloth she kept hanging on a peg driven into the wall.

"Evenin', wife," Gabriel said from the doorway, startling her.

Celia whirled around, smiling, and hurried to embrace him. He smelled of the stables, of hay and saddle soap. It was a pleasant smell. He looked over her shoulder, then pointed at the cloth bundle. "Supper?"

Celia nodded. "I got to go dress Mistress Madelaine in about half a hour. I'm sorry I can't cook somethin' up hot but the pork pie is—"

"It'll do fine," Gabriel said, cutting off her apology.

"I'm sorry I got to go back," Celia began, but he raised one hand to stop her again.

"I know you can't help it, Celia. I jus' wish you minded as much as I do. You don't."

Celia didn't answer. They had had this argument more than once. She started to work open the knots in the cloth bundle. Opening it, she saw that Lily had included the packet of goose grease she had asked for. She held it up. "For your back."

Gabriel turned and lifted his shirt. "It's been itchin' and achin' today."

Celia scooped up some of the soft grease and very gently rubbed it into the whip cuts on Gabriel's back, working her way down from his shoulders to his waist. They were closing beautifully, and none of them was red or weeping. He was going to heal clean. Gabriel still blamed Master LeBlanc, but Celia didn't see how he could, since Master had fired the overseer that same morning. But that, too, was an argument they'd had a dozen times, and she had no wish to start it again now.

"There ain't hardly even goin' to be scars," she told him. "I wish I had a lookin' glass to show you."

Gabriel let out a long breath and moved away, standing up without saying a word.

"Do you like stable work?" Celia asked him, wishing he would turn so she could see his face. But he didn't.

"It's all right," he said, looking toward the far wall. "Anything's better than breaking my back over them cane rows."

"What's wrong?" Celia asked him.

When he did turn around, she saw anger on his face. "The old man wants his sons there, not me. An' he hates me for it." Celia was quiet for a moment, unsure what to say. Before she could speak, Gabriel went on. "He tol' me to bring in a stallion that was plain-as-day wild. That horse clipped me twice kickin' and tried to get ahold of my arm the whole way in. I barely got the gate shut before he came after me."

Celia inhaled slowly. "And you think that Henry knew—"

"Celia," Gabriel interrupted her. "He knows every horse on this place. He knows whether they like oats or corn better, whether they like a soft bit or need a hard one."

"What're you saying, Gabriel?" she whispered.

"He's tryin' to get me hurt," Gabriel said flatly.

Celia caught her breath. "You could tell Master—"

"Celia!" Gabriel exploded. Then he lowered his voice. "You ain't goin' to tell Master LeBlanc, Celia. Every man on the place would surely hate me. Some of them already do. They know why I'm in them stables to begin with."

Celia shook her head. If she said Mistress Madelaine's name aloud, it would only start another argument.

"I will settle this," Gabriel whispered.

Celia felt a weight like a stone in her stomach. If she said anything to Mistress Madelaine, it would be impossible to keep her from telling her father. But how could she just let Gabriel keep working in the stables if old Henry wished him harm?

"Not a word to anyone about it, Celia," Gabriel said in a measured voice. "Not a word. Promise me on your heart."

Celia felt the stone in her stomach turn over and sink lower. "But—"

"Henry is an old man," Gabriel said. "It makes sense for him to give me the hard part of the job. I jus' have to get good at it."

Celia felt the stone lighten a little. "Can you? Without anything bad happening?"

Gabriel nodded, then shrugged. "I don't much like horses."

"They always scare me a little," Celia admitted, letting him gather her up in his arms. "They are jus' so big." She breathed the last word against his neck and felt him chuckling, laughing at how helpless and girl-

74

ish she sounded. She felt the closeness of their embrace change, and he held her tighter, then lifted her chin with his hand. She kissed him passionately, closing her mind to all the evil thoughts and fears it had been full of moments before. They loved each other so much. That was enough to make all the rest of her worries dissolve.

From the crib box, Daniel shifted and cried, and Celia drew back. They both waited, not making a sound. When the crying stopped and gentled back into sleepy sighs, Gabriel pulled her close again and whispered in her ear. "Go in and help that white woman get dressed, then, but you come back to me the minute you can."

Celia crossed the lawn, Gabriel's last kiss still warm on her mouth. The window lights were on, and the sun was sitting just on the horizon, fat and orange.

Mistress Madelaine seemed preoccupied and troubled. Celia felt guilty pretending that she didn't notice, talking along brightly as she tightened her corset, then dressed her hair. The truth was, for the first time in her life, Celia didn't want to ask what was wrong. She wished Mistress Madelaine every good thing there was in the world, but she didn't want to stay a minute longer than she had to. She wanted to be back out in her cabin with Gabriel and her son, both precious to her heart.

7

Françoise stared into the flickering campfire. He could not make himself stop picturing the lovely daughter of the manor. *Madelaine*. Her name was musical, and her grace on horseback was wonderful.

It was someone else's night to cook, and Françoise was glad. Not long after the boy's accident, Mr. Sheldon had moved them to the cornfield, to finish up a section the slaves had started but hadn't finished for some reason. It had taken less than an hour to guess why. The first snake had surprised Philippe, who had killed it with a rock. The second had been between Françoise and Paul. Françoise had pinned its head while Paul pulled his belt knife to cut it off.

It made such brutal sense that Françoise had been stunned by the logic that LeBlanc must have used to make the decision. *If a snake is going to kill a man, would you prefer it to be a man you own, so that the loss is yours,*

*or a man you can send home with friends for his funeral at
no cost to yourself?*

With Sheldon shouting at them to hurry, to work
faster, Françoise had begun yelling a warning every few
minutes. They had all taken up the cry of caution, keeping one another alert, ready, until Sheldon got tired of
competing with them and fell silent. No one had been bit-
ten. They had killed three more snakes, all cottonmouths,
all big, angry at the floods that had washed them down
out of the swamp into the cornfield to begin with.

Françoise leaned forward and spat into the fire,
thinking about the overseer's arrogance, his rude
demeanor. Mr. Sheldon was a pompous fool. Then his
thoughts drifted back to Madelaine. He had caught
one last glimpse of her toward quitting time. She rode
like the wind, her big gelding pounding along, her hat
off. Her hair was beautiful. She was beautiful. And she
had been scared for the boy. He had seen genuine
concern on her face.

Madelaine was more than a spoiled planter's daughter. He was sure of it. Françoise felt an ache in his
heart, and the painful intensity of his longing scared
him. There was no chance for this love of his to
become reality. No chance at all.

Somewhere in the dark on the other side of the fire,
Françoise heard the sound of a fiddle being tuned. He
felt his muscles begin to relax. *Bless Philippe.* He played
them to sleep most nights.

When Celia had gone, Madelaine sat alone at her
dressing table, staring into the mirror.

"Mistress Madelaine?" It was a soft, dignified voice from the hallway, and Madelaine recognized it instantly. She stood up to open the door. "Tell Maman that I will be down in a moment, please, Hope," Madelaine told the tall servant. Hope inclined her head respectfully, then turned to leave, her long steps gliding over the polished wood of the hallway floor. Madelaine watched her. Hope rarely smiled, and Madelaine realized abruptly that she had no idea why. The stately woman had belonged to Maman's Aunt Germaine and left to Maman in her will years before. *Is she like Lily? Does she have a family somewhere, lost to her forever?*

Madelaine started down the hall, her kidskin slippers making no sound at all on the hard planks of the floor. Maman had decided she should wear the chocolate-colored gown tonight even though it was too warm to have a fire. Madelaine saw, as she lifted her skirts a few inches coming down the staircase, that Maman had filled the hearth with cut flowers, the old-fashioned way.

"Oh, my, she has grown up even since we saw her in June," one of the women whispered.

Madelaine looked toward them as she came down the last step or two. She recognized one couple from Baton Rouge parties on their summer trip: Monsieur and Madame Jacques. The other man and his wife were strangers to her. The wife was squinting her eyes as though she were nearsighted. She had on an expanse of striped yellow gabardine, and it stretched tightly across her ample bosom where she bulged over the top of her corset.

"Madelaine, I am happy to present you to the Grangers," Papa said, standing as she got closer.

Madelaine stopped and bent her knees slightly, dipping into a near curtsy, her eyes lowered.

"What a charming girl," the wife said.

Madelaine smiled and dipped again.

"And this is Monsieur Jacques and his wife, Madame Jacques, as you recall."

Madelaine curtsied once more, then made her way slowly, watching her posture, to a settee wide enough to accommodate her dress. She sat down, fixing a smile on her face.

"What a lovely, commodious home you have," Madame Jacques said.

Maman made a gracious sound and a vague gesture with her hands. "I do try to make it cheerful."

"Oh, you have managed much more than that, I assure you," Madame Jacques said. Then her eyes turned to Madelaine. "And you are fortunate to have such a peerless example of homemaking to learn from, young lady."

Madelaine smiled a little wider, tilting her head the way Hope did, not answering aloud. She hoped it would have the same effect on Madame Jacques that Hope's reserve often had on strangers—they usually got less talkative and less forward. Madame Jacques continued to look at her. No one else said a word as the seconds ticked past.

"Yes," Madelaine finally responded to end the awkward silence. "I am ever so lucky to have Maman to learn from."

"Just look at the flowers in the hearth," Madame Jacques said. "That's a touch from thirty years ago. I recall my Philadelphia aunt filling her summer hearth with flowers. And she was old-fashioned to the end of her days," the woman finished, smiling.

Madelaine wasn't sure whether her mother had been paid a compliment or subtly insulted. She sat forward a little, watching Madame Jacques carefully. She had done no more than exchange pleasantries with her in Baton Rouge. Perhaps she was not as bland as the other bankers' wives Madelaine had met when they stopped to visit at Belle Grove on their way upriver to St. Louis or Memphis.

"I am wondering what you think about the nightriders," Madame Jacques said abruptly.

Her husband cleared his throat. "Lisel! Perhaps these kind folk would prefer not to—"

"Oh!" she interrupted him, then shrugged, her face earnest. "I apologize for being so abrupt, but I do wonder, Monsieur LeBlanc."

Madelaine leaned forward, watching her father. He had looked angry for a second, then his face smoothed. "I think perhaps we should—"

"What is a nightrider?" Madelaine interrupted him to ask. She held her breath, hoping he would answer, that the conversation could *mean* something for a change, that someone would want to talk about something that mattered. She turned charmingly, feeling the stays in her corset dig into the tops of her thighs. "Please, Papa?"

He looked out the window at the far end of the

room, then up at the ceiling, then he met Madelaine's eyes. "They are vigilantes. They have been trying to rid the countryside of the criminal element."

Madelaine sat back, nonplussed. She had expected something to do with secession and the threat of war. "Criminals?"

"There are so many ne'er-do-wells," Maman put in.

Mr. Granger rubbed his hand across his forehead. "We hear terrible things down in New Orleans," he said. "Hangings and beatings. Judge Lynch and his followers do scare the ladies."

"They say there is the question of a slave rebellion," Mrs. Granger put in. She shook her head. "But I suppose you are used to that."

Madelaine saw her mother nod, a tiny, almost imperceptible motion. Madelaine felt her heart speed up. Papa had the oddest expression on his face. "That has little to do with the vigilance committees, though, as I am sure you understand."

"And the stories are no doubt exaggerated," Mr. Granger said quietly, patting his wife's hand reassuringly.

"None of them is getting any more than he deserves, I am sure," Papa said evenly. "Though I cannot pretend to know much about it." Then he stood up, gesturing for them all to rise. "I want to show you my wife's roses," he announced.

Everyone stood. Madelaine saw Monsieur Jacques catch his wife's eyes, severe reproval on his face. Whatever the nightriders were, Madelaine thought, he was angry at his wife for bringing them up. She stole a glance at her father. Papa's face was a mask of genial blandness as they walked out the double doors onto the lawn. Madelaine sighed. Three minutes of real conversation, and the rest of the evening would be spent saying nothing at all, she was sure of it.

It was cooling off outside, and she glanced westward. The sun would be setting in minutes. Madelaine picked up her skirts and daintily made her way across the garden paths toward the rose beds. Her head was spinning. She longed to ask Madame Jacques so many things about the nightriders, about the possibility of war. Maybe she would finally get some answers.

A barely audible whistle made Madelaine look around. The conversation between Maman and the ladies was focused now on layering perpetual hybrids and whether or not cow manure was too rich a fertilizer for tea roses, and it swirled on without her. She blinked. Then the whistle came again, a silvery six-note melody this time.

Madelaine's eyes followed the sound, and she spotted the tall Cajun man standing at the edge of the peach orchard. He was back far enough in the trees so that someone who hadn't noticed the whistle—and without it to guide their eyes—would never see him. But as Madelaine stared, he raised one hand in a gesture of greeting, then stepped backward and out of sight.

"What do you think about the Noisettes, Madelaine?" Mrs. Granger was asking. "Do you enjoy them as much as the Bourbon roses? I love the Madame Angelina's, that pure lovely cream-white."

She tried to answer but hated to turn, to look away.

"Madelaine?" Maman's voice was sharp.

Madelaine spun around, startled out of her daze. Her slippers skidded on the damp grass. Her father shot out a hand and steadied her. "You're flushed," he said, looking into her face. "Are you well?"

Madelaine nodded. "Perfectly," she managed, then half turned to steal a last glance at the place where the Cajun man had stood. Her heart was pounding, and she could feel the warmth radiating from her cheeks.

"Madelaine?" her father said quietly.

"I am just a little warm, that's all." She said it without turning for another few seconds, hoping her cheeks were not as pink as they felt.

"It's cooler out here than in the house," Maman said cheerfully, scrutinizing Madelaine.

"Do you use the *Housekeeper's Encyclopedia?*" Madame Jacques was asking Maman. "Bless Mrs. Haskell, she has the best receipt for rosehip sauce. Not so sweet as most."

"Watch your footing," Papa said gently, then released Madelaine's arm.

The men drifted off in a loose knot, talking in low voices. The women's conversation went on, veering from roses to the best way to make use of the new French fabrics that were coming into the New Orleans ports. Madelaine half listened, glancing back at the orchard a dozen times as the merits of different dressmakers were discussed, with Maman insisting that for lighter cloth the French seamstresses were not to be equaled.

As they started back, slowly crossing the wide lawn, Madelaine knew she should tell her father, but she also felt a strange sense of complacency about what had happened. The Cajun man meant her no harm, she felt sure of that. He had probably just been walking through the orchard and heard the voices from the lawn. He was good-hearted, she was sure. No man who stepped forward so quickly to help an injured boy was capable of harm.

Rory Quinn had never felt better in his life. The night was cool, and the moon was bright, a beacon on the horizon. His blood was up, the exhilaration of the ride still with him. The others all had split off on their separate ways home except for Sheldon, who was married but not much older than Rory himself.

Rory still could feel the kind of shiver low in his spine that usually came with hunting snakes. They had taken two of the Lafouche Parish's worst to see Judge Lynch this night, and he was not sorry, nor would he ever be. The world was better off without scoundrels like the two they had hung.

One of the men had come out shooting. Rory had risked his life rushing him from the side, knocking the gun from his hand. He dragged in another deep breath of the sweet night air. It had been an impulse, and he knew he was lucky not to have been killed. "Probably best LeBlanc had bankers to entertain tonight," Sheldon said, riding up beside him, spitting into the road, then turning back. The deep shadows made a gargoyle of the man's face, twisting his grin into something grotesque.

Rory looked away, pulling in another deep breath. "Why is that?"

"He never wants to just hang them and get it over with," Sheldon said.

Rory shrugged, holding in his mare. She tossed her head, fighting the pressure on the reins. Maybe it was wrong, hanging men like that without a proper trial, but at least the two were out of commission forever. There would never be another swindle out of either one of them. Their wives would never be bruised black and blue again. Nor would their neighbors find a pig missing once or twice a year.

"This parish is goin' to thank us all one fine day," Sheldon said evenly.

Rory nodded, his breath still quick, as though he had been running. "What's LeBlanc's daughter like?" Rory asked.

Sheldon touched his lips lightly with his fingertips. "Beautiful, kind-hearted. Skin like peaches. Why?"

"I've been invited for Sunday supper. I have a feeling the old man wants me to like her."

"You will," Sheldon told him. "Any man would. Go home and count your blessings."

Rory nodded, then he threw back his head and pulled in a huge breath. The levee road was empty ahead of them. Without thinking about why he was doing it, or if he should, he shouted at the sky. A long, wordless shout of wild triumph.

After a few seconds, Sheldon joined in, and they bayed at the moon like two wolves, standing high in their stirrups, their horses fidgeting and prancing beneath them.

Rory was the first to break into sharp-edged laughter. On an impulse, he threw his weight forward, giving the mare her head. Already nervous and dancing, she exploded into a gallop. Sheldon took only a moment to react, urging his tall bay into a gallop. In an instant, they were racing flat-out along the levee road in the moonlight, shouting taunts and jibes at each other like schoolboys. Rory could feel his own pulse roaring in his temples as his mare drew into the lead and held it.

Françoise heard the plantation bell tolling before he heard the overseer's shout. Men around him straightened up, and he joined them in the groaning stretch that accompanied the end of every day's work. He brushed at the sweat on his forehead with his sleeve, then stuck the long cane knife into the soft soil and looked up. The overseer, the arrogant little man named Sheldon, was riding the line with his usual officious manner. Françoise glanced down the line and caught Philippe's eye. They shared an intent look. Neither could stand Sheldon.

"As many of you as will work on Sunday are welcome again this week," the overseer shouted as he rode up and down the line of workers. The sun sparkled off the slender cane leaves as a whirling breeze crossed the wide, flat field.

"*Moi? Non,*" an older man named Alfonse muttered from behind Françoise. Françoise tried not to smile. Alfonse had been talking about quitting since the first day of work but hadn't done it yet. He had come the last two Sundays, too.

"How many?" the overseer was shouting. He lifted his whip to point to the west. "The next field over was planted later, and it's still light-stalked. It'll be easier to set up than it has been to strip and cut. After that, we'll be finished. Another week's work, through next Sunday, probably, then that's it." He paused, then lifted his chin. "So? Sunday workers?"

There was a ragged show of hands. Françoise turned to see. Philippe was among them. They all wanted to make the wages before the work dried up. Françoise was glad Philippe would stay. He was the only man among the crew who was a neighbor. To live among this many strangers was strange, and Françoise didn't like it. He preferred his bayou, where he was surrounded by family and friends.

"Higher!" the overseer shouted, as though they had offended him somehow. Françoise raised his hand over his head along with the others, but for a blinding second he wanted to drag the overseer off his horse and beat him until he apologized to every man here for the last three weeks of badgering and rudeness.

Françoise squinted up at the sky, anger seething beneath his skin. This had to be a small dose of what the slaves felt. Surely they fought this rage every minute of their lives. They would have to. A slave who lifted so much as a finger against his master was doomed.

"That's twenty-two of you," Mr. Sheldon yelled at them, as though the number were pitiful—even though it was the majority. "I'll count again tomorrow, so look around and make note of who-all is promising to come. Broken promises will be remembered Monday morning. Some of you will be kind enough to help me with that, I am sure."

Astounded, Françoise looked down to keep the overseer from seeing his face. The man was saying he expected them to give him the names of friends and neighbors who had promised Sunday work and who changed their minds. *Why? So he can refuse to hire them back on Monday? Or will their pay be docked?* There had already been three men whose pay had been cut because they took firewood out of the orchard one chilly night. No one was sure how the overseer had found out who had done it, but it was obvious that someone had told him.

Françoise took a deep breath. He would not be here much longer. If plantation owners felt they could charge their laborers for firewood—when the orchards had windrows of deadwood piled up and rotting—they were as greed-possessed as Antoine always said they were. Mr. Sheldon had informed them the following morning that any firewood they would need for cooking and for safety at night would have to come from the swamp. Françoise clenched his fists, remembering the morning Sheldon had lectured them like children about it.

Monsieur LeBlanc was shrewd. Firewood dragged out of the swamp cleared his land for him, kept the smaller bayous and canal from getting choked with deadfalls. Why not figure a way to have the work done for free by men already tired from a day's work?

"I will see you half an hour before sunup, then,"

Mr. Sheldon shouted, cupping his hands around his mouth to make sure all could hear him at once.

Françoise looked up and down the line of workers. The faces all looked tired, dirty, and impatient for the day's work to end. As Sheldon rode off, Françoise found himself staring after the man, knowing he should probably quit now, tonight, draw his wages Monday morning, and never come back again. He hated working like this, at someone else's beck and call, under someone else's rules. On top of everything else about this place that grated on him, what they were doing to the cane was wrong, to his way of thinking.

Instead of trimming it and laying it in the furrows for the sugarhouse gangs to pick up and process, they should be setting the stalks back up. The cane had been flattened, but most had good strong roots still in the soil. In two more months, the cane would make twice the syrup it was going to make now. It would recover, he was sure of it, but instead they were chopping it down, stripping it for the grinder.

Françoise picked up his cane knife and stripped one more stalk, using four quick strokes. The first cut it from the plant, two more slashes trimmed the leaves from one side, then the other. Then, with a flourish, he lopped off the tufted top. He laid the trimmed cane in the furrow, then walked to the edge of the field.

Wearily, he added his knife to the pile already left there. No one forgot to turn in his knife. Not since Sheldon had come riding into their camp that second night, cursing and frantic because one was missing.

The man who had brought the long-bladed knife back to sharpen it as he sat before the fire had handed it over, as astounded as the rest of them.

Françoise turned to follow the straggling line of men heading back to the camp. He had thought about quitting often. But every day or two, he would manage to get a glimpse of the lovely Madelaine. "And her father will have you driven off the place if he notices," Françoise muttered to himself. But he knew the danger didn't matter to him as much as the possibility of seeing Madelaine. He wanted to talk to her. He wanted desperately for her heart to be as lovely as the rest of her.

Halfway to camp, Françoise heard hoofbeats. His heart lifting, he saw a rider cantering along the road in the dusk. The silhouette of slender waist and billowing skirts left little doubt who it was. For a long moment, Françoise just looked at her. Then he began to whistle a quick-noted tune—a fiddle tune he had learned from his mother.

In the dimming light, the girl reined in. She turned her horse toward him but stayed on the road. He couldn't see her face clearly; the light was failing fast.

"You really do sound like some imaginary bird," she called.

He grinned at her. "My *maman* was a bird, singing, whistling, always happy as she worked."

"Do you sing, too?" she asked.

He nodded. "I do. Do you dance?"

He could see her smile in spite of the dusk. "I do love dancing if the floor isn't too crowded. I play the piano, but I am shy as violets about it. Do you know anything about war coming?"

"I know what I hear," he said, surprised at the question.

"Tell me," she said, and he could hear an intensity in her voice that puzzled him.

A second set of hoofbeats made Françoise's heart ache. Madelaine turned her horse, but not in time. He could hear her father scolding her as they rode off. ". . . so far below your station," came Monsieur LeBlanc's sharp voice. Then no more.

Françoise watched them go. Then he headed toward the flicker of the campfire that had been built. He lengthened his stride, acutely aware of how dirty and sweaty he was, how ragged his work clothes had become. There was so little time left. Seven or eight more days.

And then he would never see her again.

8

"Go upstairs and dress," Maman was saying. "Celia should be here any moment." Madelaine nodded, trying not to be ill-tempered, but the truth was, she was upset with her father.

"He really was harsh with me last night," she said again. But Maman was already shaking her head.

"He had every right. You have no business talking to a hired field man, Madelaine."

"You should hear him whistling, Maman. It's just like a flute." *And he has deep blue eyes and a wonderful smile*, she thought, but said nothing aloud. *He makes me feel beautiful.* She felt her cheeks flush at the thought and pretended to study her fingernails. They were clipped in little arches like half moons—the new style from Paris.

"I have no doubt this man is the finest whistler ever born into Lafouche Parish," Maman said. Madelaine glanced back and saw a smile twitching at her mother's lips. "But you still had no reason to address a field hand."

Madelaine shook her head but said nothing, still feeling warmth in her cheeks. She knew her mother was right—or, at least, that most of the people she knew would agree. But it seemed ridiculous to her. The man had done nothing wrong, nor had she. He had been polite and cordial, nothing more. "You never lectured about this when I was younger," she said very quietly, remembering the many times she and Celia had played in the quarter with all the other children—until someone found her and brought her home.

Maman was arching her brows. "When you were younger, there was little reason to expect you to act like a young lady. Now there is every reason to expect it."

"But Maman, Papa was coming up right behind me. I knew he was there, that I was properly escorted. It was just like that first time. There was no danger at all. And no impropriety." Madelaine rushed the words out, then took a breath.

"There are certain things a respectable woman does not do," Maman said flatly into the silence. "Speaking to strange men—especially men below one's own station in life—is foolish and unladylike."

Madelaine caught her breath, trying to find the perfect response, the answer that would make her mother see that this man was not a threat to her in any way. He was more polite than her brothers' friends had been, always teasing her and saying things that made her blush. And she just knew he was gentle.

"There are things we do because it is how they have

always been done," Maman was saying. "Proper forms of address—or not addressing certain people—remind everyone of their place in the scheme of things, Madelaine."

Madelaine didn't answer. Maman insisted on Celia calling her Mistress Madelaine, always, whether anyone else was around or not. No argument could ever persuade her it was silly. When they had been about twelve, Madelaine had tried to get Celia to stop, just to call her by her name, but by then Celia herself had balked. Madelaine had not understood then, but she did now. Celia had been afraid that if she had gotten out of the habit, she'd forget someday in the presence of Madelaine's parents or some guest. And then she would have been punished.

"Madelaine!" Maman broke into her thoughts. "It is time for you to begin dressing. I don't want you late coming down to greet our guest."

"It makes no sense," Madelaine said quietly, knowing she was close to starting a real argument and not sure why. "I should be able to make a simple remark to anyone I please so long as he does nothing improper."

"There are rules one lives by," Maman said heavily.

"I can't see why Celia has to call me Mistress, either," Madelaine went on recklessly. "I'm her friend. You are her mistress, Maman, not I. I think it is wrong to own slaves."

"Madelaine!" Maman said in a harsh voice. "I hope you have never whispered such nonsense to Celia. You will ruin that girl and make her life miserable. I am ashamed of you!"

Madelaine lowered her eyes. "Shoo," Maman said, waving her hands. "You are provoking me simply to rebel, and I do not find it appropriate, especially with a guest in the house. You have less than an hour, and I want you to look wonderful." Her face was bleak and stern.

Madelaine didn't want to apologize, but she knew if she didn't, Maman would be angry all evening. "I'm sorry," she said. She *was* sorry she had upset her mother. She was not apologizing for her growing conviction that slavery was wrong. Maman murmured something conciliatory and patted her cheek, then left the room.

Celia came in through the back door, tucking her hair beneath her scarf. Gabriel had been upset about her having to come back tonight, but he was beginning to say less about it, and she was glad. With him in the stables and her in the big house, they could be doing very well for themselves as time went on. There would be leftovers and extra food for Daniel, too, and he could learn horse sense and stable work as he grew up and never go to the fields at all—if they were lucky.

"I think Mistress Madelaine is already upstairs," Lily said from her baking table.

Celia nodded, looking past her. "Pies?"

Lily nodded. "Peach. It's the last of those windfalls we picked up."

"Gabriel loves peach pie," Celia said, and smiled.

Lily laughed. "You are purely spoiled, aren't you, chile?"

Celia hesitated, but Lily was smiling good-naturedly.

"If there is some left and Mistress says it is all right, Gabriel would be forever grateful," she told Lily. "He says the bes' day this year was the day you came to take over this kitchen."

Lily's smile widened, and Celia was glad. Maybe her sorrow was lifting a little. Celia hoped so.

"There you are," Mistress LeBlanc said as Celia stepped into the hallway that ran past the parlor.

Celia nodded, hoping she was not going to get in trouble for being a few minutes late. But Mistress only waved her past.

"I just sent Madelaine up, Celia. She is bound to be nervous, so see if you can calm her down a little."

Celia nodded. "Yes, ma'am. I will."

"We count on you, Celia," Mistress said, and Celia felt a little flush of pride.

Madelaine watched Celia fuss at the dressing table. She wanted more than anything to talk to Celia, to try to understand her heart. Once Madelaine had begun thinking about slavery, about what it must mean to be enslaved, to have all choices taken away, she had realized something terrible. Deep down, Celia must hate her. And the idea broke Madelaine's heart. She could see Celia tense whenever she so much as hinted at any of this, and that made her even sadder.

"She expects me to fit all of you into this?" Celia said from beside the dressing table. She was holding up the corset Maman had brought in earlier. Madelaine laughed aloud, and Celia let the hourglass-shaped corset swing obscenely from her fingertips. "Mistress

Madelaine, a ten-year-old child is not this small through the middle. We are goin' to need four or five tightenings."

Madelaine laughed again, a warm relief coursing through her as Celia joked, her eyes twinkling as they always had. "I won't be able to eat much," she admitted.

Celia arched her brows. "You ain't gonna be able to *breathe.*"

Madelaine smiled. "Do you remember that day we tried to dress you all up and the corset made you squeal?"

Celia nodded, her eyes shining, and Madelaine knew she was remembering the days when they had played together without thinking much about anything except making each other giggle. Madelaine hugged her, and Celia embraced her warmly without hesitation, then they stood apart for a few seconds, looking into each other's eyes. "Whatever happens," Madelaine said deliberately, "whatever changes, whatever tears the world apart, we will be friends."

"Oh, I do hope so," Celia said, and for a few seconds, Madelaine could see all the way into her eyes—all the caution had been momentarily erased. She tried to smile and found herself crying. Celia's eyes flooded, too, and then they hugged again.

"Are you dressing?"

Maman's voice made them spring apart, wiping their cheeks.

"Oh, don't come in," Madelaine called out, sounding breathless and hoping her mother would assume she was only nervous about meeting Rory. "I want to surprise you."

"I've thought of somethin' new to do for her hair, Mistress," Celia added. They exchanged a nervous glance.

"All right. But don't try anything too silly," Maman said through the closed door. She laughed gently. "This will be a nice evening, Madelaine, just enjoy yourself."

Madelaine waited until her mother's footsteps faded, then she looked at Celia. "Do you have a new idea for my hair?"

Celia shook her head. "I'd surely better get one now." They both laughed.

Henry stepped out through the stable door to glare at the dusky sky. Gabriel had gone home for the night, and he was alone. Sunset was a time he usually prized. But tonight was different. All his joints were aching, usually a sign of a storm coming. And if it did come, he was ill prepared for it. The last month of fine weather had lulled him into laziness. There were three mares in the field that were close to foaling—too close if the storm turned out to be anything beyond a little light rain. They were not likely to get another bad one—nothing like last time, anyway—but Henry knew he would be in for real trouble if anything happened to the mares that were heavy with foal. They had lost foals after the last storm. If he left mares out and it happened again . . .

Henry sighed. The stars were coming out, and it was clear as a bell. "There ain't goin' to be no storm," he said aloud, willing himself to believe it. It might be true. There were nights now when his bones ached for no reason at all. Still, he stood looking up at the sky.

"Damn it all," he said aloud. "I shoulda had Gabriel do it earlier."

Angry with himself, Henry clenched his fists. It was equally true that Gabriel should have thought to bring the mares in on his own. He wasn't thinking like a horseman yet, and there was no indication that he ever would.

"I ain't s'posed to have to tell him," Henry muttered, working up his anger at Gabriel, liking it much better than his anger at himself. That was it. He had thought that Gabriel would bring the mares into the foaling stalls. By the time he had noticed it hadn't been done, it was pitch dark and storming.

Henry chuckled to himself at the perfect shape of the plan. If there was no storm, he would be fine. And if there was, he would be fine, too. It'd be Gabriel in trouble. Maybe that'd be enough to make Master LeBlanc realize he had the wrong man in the job. Henry was still smiling when the sound of hammering hoofbeats made him squint down the orchard road.

Rory Quinn had pulled his mare to a halt at the gates. A lantern had been uncovered, and a deep voice had called out.

"Master Quinn?"

"I am he," Rory answered, and the gate swung open.

"They are 'specting you up at the big house, Master Quinn," the servant told him, his voice polite and welcoming.

"Which way are the stables?" Rory asked.

"I can take your mare up there from the house if you like, sir," the servant said.

Rory sized the man up. He was tall and strong-looking and not old. But none of that meant he was a horseman, and this mare was a handful. It would be a fine hospitality gift if one of Monsieur LeBlanc's prize slaves ended up with a broken leg tonight. "I think I will ride her myself. Which way is the stable?"

The servant raised the lantern to gesture down the levee. "Up just a little stretch, then turn off on the lane that has them two big old magnolias on either side. Just follow straight on through the orchards. I'll send someone to bring you on up to the big house from there, sir."

"Thank you," Rory said absently, holding the mare in check long enough to make sure that the servant was out of the way. Then he let her have her head and cantered down the levee road.

The magnolias were old and magnificent, their branches touching above the road to form an arch of broad black leaves against the sky. The road between them was straight and smooth. There were marks down the center where the drag box had been run over it in the past day or two, so Rory let the mare canter again. A flash of lightning on the horizon startled her into a gallop, and he pulled her slowly back in hand.

A second distant flash revealed the ghostly outline of barn buildings and corrals up ahead. Rory held the mare steady this time and smiled. If a storm came in and kept him here a few days, so much the better. His father had spent heavily to buy the new bagasse-burning boilers for the sugarhouse and had had new syrup vats and cypress hogsheads made up as well. Since the hurricane, he had been in a state, frantic to make sure that the smaller cotton and yam crops didn't fail, too. Rory could not understand his father's fear. There was no shortage of loan money in New Orleans this year.

Rory couldn't wait to take over the plantation. He would do things differently, take some risks. He'd spend money on something besides new sugarhouse machinery. There were small fortunes won and lost at every race meeting. He would travel to England, buy a foundation sire or two. Then he would import mares from the Arabs. The smartest horsemen were doing that now, and the crossed blood was making for some fine animals.

Enjoying the daydream of being lord of his own manor, Rory pulled the mare back, slowing her steadily so that by the time he was close enough to see the old groom standing out in front of the stables, lantern in hand, he had the mare almost to a dancing walk, her head high and her shoulders lathered.

The servant stepped forward to hold the mare still while Rory dismounted. "Evenin', sir." Rory could hear his advanced age in the hoarseness and unsteadiness of his voice, even though he couldn't see him clearly.

"Good evening, Uncle," Rory said, returning the pleasantry. "Can you point the way to the big house?"

"Yes, sir," the stableman said. "Jus' follow the

orchard road on around. You come up on the side lawns and the rose gardens."

"Walk her cool." Rory handed him the reins, and the lightning flashed once again. This time, he could hear the faint roll of thunder. "Then dry her with a good rubdown. Make sure she doesn't catch a chill. This mare is important to me."

"Yes, sir," the stableman answered.

Rory hesitated but knew LeBlanc wasn't likely to have a fool in charge of his stables. The mare would be in good hands.

"This way?" Rory asked a second time, pointing. "Do you have another lantern I can take?"

The old man led his mare inside, and Rory waited for him to light a second lantern. Rory had gone only a hundred yards up the road when he felt a spatter of cool rain on his face as the wind rushed past, then died down again. Lightning sparkled on the southern horizon.

With a sense of relief, it occurred to him that there would be no night rides if a storm came in. That last night, the hanging, his shouting on the levee . . . it had all come back to bother him more than once. He wasn't exactly ashamed of what he had done, but his reaction to it had disturbed him.

"Rain, then," he said aloud, looking up at the sky. Lightning threaded across the southern sky as if it had heard him, and he almost smiled. It probably would pour for a few days. It was September fourteenth, after all, well into the storm season. If Miss LeBlanc was as pretty as Sheldon had said, and her father set a good table, this could be a very pleasant visit.

9

Madelaine straightened her back. Standing perfectly erect was the only possible position in a corset this tight-laced.

"Is it all right, Mistress?" Celia asked. "S'pose you can tolerate it?"

Madelaine nodded and smoothed the wine-colored cloth of the gown against her bosom and belly and turned sideways, looking in the mirror. She had to admit that the gown fit better with this corset, draping without a hint of pull or pinch. And the long fringe on the cream-colored lace wrap swung gracefully with her every movement. She glanced at her bed. Four other wraps lay draped on the rail. "Do you think the gold-threaded one looked better?"

Celia shook her head, and Madelaine scrutinized her face. Sometimes Celia got tired of offering her opinion and ceased to have one. "You look beautiful, Mistress Madelaine," Celia breathed, and her face was sincere, almost rapt. Madelaine felt instantly contrite. Celia knew how important this evening was, or how important it *could* be.

Madelaine stared at herself in the mirror, trying to ignore her uneasy stomach. Beautiful? Her nose was too small, and her eyes were too big. She looked like a ten-year-old market waif except for the gorgeous dress and Celia's intricate pile of arranged curls. "My hair does," she told Celia. "Thank you for that." She reached out, and Celia embraced her quickly, then stepped back, respectful of the gown's voluminous folds. Madelaine smiled apologetically at her for even trying to hug.

The mirror drew Madelaine's attention once again, and she turned toward it, her eyes meeting Celia's in the reflection. "I wonder what he'll be like," Madelaine whispered.

"Handsome and kind," Celia said. "That's what I am hoping for."

Madelaine smiled at her, then saw in the mirror that she was forgetting everything her mother had taught her and showing all her teeth like a little girl. Her smile faded. "But he will probably be unhandsome and dull and frowning," she said aloud.

Celia reached out and touched her cheek gently. "Maybe not. Maybe he'll be jus' plain wonderful."

Madelaine took a little breath and felt herself blushing. Celia took her hand and squeezed it tightly. "He'd be some fool not to fall in love with you."

Madelaine blinked back tears. "You are always so kind to me," she said, then cleared her throat and daubed at her eyes with a handkerchief from her dressing table. There was a low rumble from outside, and it took Madelaine a moment to realize what it was.

"Oh, Celia," she said. "I won't be able to stay up here much longer. Mother will never allow me to——"

"I'll be jus' fine," Celia said, but her voice sounded hollow.

"If it gets too stormy, go back out, and Gabriel will hold your hand," Madelaine said. Celia shook her head stubbornly.

Madelaine took Celia's shoulders and forced her to meet her eyes. "Yes. If Hope or Lily has to help me undress, it won't hurt a thing. I'll tell Maman something."

Celia looked askance out the window as the sound of thunder rumbled again, a little louder this time.

"I will tell her that I insisted you go. That you argued with me and I told you I was ordering you to do it," Madelaine added.

Celia looked relieved. "Thank you."

Madelaine embraced Celia, another quick hug that barely touched their cheeks over the wide hoops of her dress. The window frame lit brightly with another flash of lightning. "You should just go now."

Celia pulled in an uneven breath and shook her head. "I'll go when you do."

Madelaine hesitated, then nodded. That was fairest. Then, neither of them would have to be alone and scared. Her stomach was literally churning, she was so nervous. She held out her hand, and Celia took it. They both stood, facing the mirror. After a moment or two,

Celia began fussing with her hair again. Madelaine closed her eyes at the familiar, comforting touch.

Rory noticed the dim glow of smokestacks in the distance—the bloom of rising smoke in the eerie glow of moonlit steam. The boilers were still going full bore even at night, then. Monsieur LeBlanc worked his plantation seriously.

The peach orchard had a pleasant, sweet scent. Rory walked carefully, not wanting to soil his boots too badly before he walked on fine carpets. At least there were no mud puddles. That meant there had been road crews working as well as the harvest going on. That meant Monsieur LeBlanc had enough labor to really take care of the place. He had two sons in France, Rory knew, so there was no question of Madelaine inheriting the whole place. But they were French, and that meant she would get some portion of its value.

"It hardly matters," Rory said to the sky as another flash of lightning winked to life, then disappeared. And he meant it. His mother was French, but he was the eldest of his Irish father's sons. He had seen the will. When it came to inheritances, his family was definitely *not* French. He would inherit everything, and his brothers would have to find trades or seek their fortunes elsewhere—or settle for working for him the rest of their lives. He would help all three of them any way he found reasonable, of course.

As he came around a curve in the road, Rory saw a lantern coming from the other direction. He cleared his throat, and the lantern carrier stopped.

"Sir?" a deep male voice called out. "I have come to light your way."

Rory blinked, startled. This was no servant's voice. This was the educated French accent of the master of the plantation.

"I thank you, Monsieur," Rory replied, and walked toward his host.

Françoise was tired. His back ached a little. And he was tired of listening to these men wrangle about the war. He cleared his throat. "But that is what will bring it, Philippe," Françoise said. "The Cajuns know nothing at all except that Mouton is their own, and they have been listening to him for forty years, and he tells them he wants secession."

There was a murmur among the others. The plates lay on the grass now, each man's his own to wash, or not, as he chose. Françoise had cooked. He was among those favored with the chore, a compliment. The gumbo had been good this night, but not as good as it could have been. The roux had been hurried, the flour browning too fast. He had stirred the sizzling fat while Philippe started the onions and meat browning in a second pan. No one had talked much until they had eaten. Sheldon had kept them working late.

The lightning was coming closer, and it looked as if it might storm. Françoise wondered if he should go find Sheldon and ask where they were to take shelter if it stormed hard. The sugarhouse wasn't far, if it came to that. There were slave crews working nearly all night now. "Do you think the Yankees will fight?" Françoise said aloud, without raising his eyes from the campfire flames. "Will they? To end slavery? I can only admire that if it is true."

"But it will have nothing to do with us in the backwaters," Philippe said flatly. Françoise knew his neighbor well. Philippe loved to argue a point—any point.

Someone else laughed aloud. "That is what your great-grandfather thought in Acadia, you fool. France, Britain, the winner won't matter to us." Everyone laughed.

"He was probably loaded onto the boat one dark night telling everyone not to worry." Françoise could not see the speaker's face, he was standing back from the fire. Everyone laughed again. Then there was an uneasy silence as each one thought about the *gran derangement*. No one wanted to believe anything like it could ever happen again. But it could. They all knew it. If they got caught in the middle the way they had in Nova Scotia, they could end up enslaved, indentured against their will, killed, their families separated for generations or forever.

Philippe was the one to break the silence, staring into the fire. "My great grandfather and grandmother died on the British ships. Different ships," he added.

"Alone, then," a man said quietly. He was young and lived south on the bayou somewhere. Françoise couldn't remember his name. He worked hard and never complained.

"You have babies?" Philippe asked.

The young man nodded. "Two. I would die to protect them."

"Imagine how the *esclave* feels," someone behind Françoise said. "For each of them, it is a continuing hell. Them, their children, their grandchildren, and no way out."

Françoise turned to nod at the tall, thin-shouldered man who had spoken. He was grateful that someone had said it aloud. He had been thinking it. How could he not think such things when his mother had been of mixed blood?

"If the slave owners get their way, there will be no freemen," Françoise said aloud. "Acadian, Creole, or English, the *bave* do not care what color their slaves are, you know. If they could use us, they would. You all see Monsieur Sheldon, the way he looks at us. If these Yankees come, and do not win . . .

"Will you fight?" Françoise asked, not expecting anyone to answer the question. "Alongside Yankees? Or alongside men who would buy and sell you if they could?"

"I am just going to stay home," Philippe said. "And hope that they fight each other and not us."

"And the rest of you?" Françoise asked the others. There was a general shuffling of feet as men sat up straighter.

"Mouton will want us to fight with him," the young man said.

"Mouton is a general, and he is a Cajun, but he is not a king," Françoise said bluntly. "From what I can hear, it sounds as though we should fight for the *Yanquis*. At least they want to end the slavery."

"But where will the slaves go if they are freed?" the thin man asked.

Françoise shrugged. "Wherever they wish."

This caused another uneasy silence among the men. Françoise knew what they were thinking. If there were hundreds of thousands of free black men trying to find land and work, there would be little left for anyone else. Would they make *pirogues* and fish the waters in the bayous? Was there enough room for them and their children in the swamps, too? They would not be rich, not for generations, anyway. They would need *petites habitats* of their own.

Françoise said nothing. He had no ready answer. There were more slaves in this part of Louisiana than white people of any kind, German, Creole, French, Irish, or English, all added together. Far more. If they were free to do what they wished, things would change. It would be far better for them, of course. And it would be *right*. But who could tell what it would mean for the others who lived here?

"Slavery is wrong in the eyes of God," the tall man said quietly. No one answered except to nod. No one could deny it. Not these men, anyway. Too many knew the stories of men and women who had been stacked up like firewood in ships' holds, no room to breathe, no way to get out of the filth on ships—just as the Africans had been. And most of them hated the planters because they had gotten rich on land that had once belonged to Cajuns.

"If this Lincoln is not elected, perhaps nothing bad will happen," Philippe said. There were sounds of assent from around the fire.

Françoise stood up and brushed at his dirty

trousers. "I am going to walk off my supper," he murmured to anyone who might want an explanation, then turned and ambled away from the campfire. He kept going in an almost straight line, heading for the stables as long as he thought anyone could see him. Then he veered, crossing the creek above the cow sheds to head toward the big house. He knew it was worse than foolish. But in all this talk of hatred and war and the painful grind of the work he had been doing, a glimpse of the girl might make it so that he could fall asleep tonight believing that there was something good in the world.

As he walked, inhaling the sweet scent of the peach trees, he let his mind drift into a pleasant daydream of dancing with Madelaine. She loved to dance, she had said. He smiled. She might be a planter's daughter, a man who sounded as though his French had come from Europe, not Acadia, but she was a Cajun at heart, he was sure of it. She was used to fine things, but he had a strong feeling that she didn't need them the way some plantation women did. She would prefer treasures of the heart if she had to choose.

Françoise shook his head and chuckled, mocking himself for making up the girl the way he wanted her to be, a fantasy without any bearing on fact or even a wisp of logic. He had no idea what she was, beyond heavenly beautiful.

The sound of men's voices made him halt abruptly, then stand as still as stone. The men were laughing politely, their voices quiet and cordial. Françoise stepped toward the shadowy peach trees, his heartbeat like a startled rabbit's. Then he realized they were moving away from him. They were walking toward the big house, too. Cautiously, he bent over and pulled off his boots, tucking them under one arm. The men ahead of him were talking steadily now. As he listened, their voices rose, and they laughed together.

Françoise whistled soundlessly between his teeth. One of the voices he thought he knew: Monsieur LeBlanc. The other belonged to a younger man, a stranger. Without letting his thoughts go any further, Françoise felt his stomach tighten.

He took one step, then another, the cool wet soil of the road molding to the soles of his feet. The rain would erase his tracks. And the sound of a man's own voice was the best cover anyone following him could have.

Gabriel watched the tracings of lightning getting closer. Daniel stirred in his crib box and whimpered as the thunder rolled.

"You ain't gonna be scared of it like your mama, are you?" Gabriel asked his son, picking him up out of his bed.

Daniel focused on his father's face and smiled his toothless smile.

"Is that so?" Gabriel pretended to scold in a singsong voice. "Is that so?"

Daniel smiled wider and made a burbling sound.

Gabriel laughed aloud. Then the sky flashed and crackled overhead, and he stopped. Celia would be terrified. And shaking. And he could not even go ask after her—not at the big house on a night they had company. Gabriel settled Daniel back in his crib and listened to him whimpering. He was hungry, but he would just have to wait until his mama could escape the clutches of that silly-minded white girl. Gabriel felt the familiar pressure of his anger and exhaled. It would do him no good at all; it could do him great harm.

"Truth is, she will be in that house until eleven or even midnight," Gabriel said aloud. He blinked against the blue-white flash of the next bolt of lightning and thought about old Henry at the stables. The old man would be walking the aisles calming the horses in the stalls. There were several mares real close to foaling. . . .

Gabriel caught his breath. The mares were all in the lower pastures, and Henry didn't like that long path, even in daylight. Would he go bring the mares up? Had he already? Gabriel patted Daniel's back absently. Surely Henry would have brought the mares in. Why wouldn't he? If anything happened to them, the master would be furious.

"At both of us," Gabriel said aloud, working the idea around in his mind. He wanted to be here in case Celia made her way out, running terrified through the storm. But if the mares were out, Henry would be in deep trouble. *And as much as he resents me,* Gabriel thought, *he might just try to pass that trouble along if he can.*

Gabriel frowned, suddenly sure. Henry would leave the mares out and hope for the best. And if the worst came instead, he would pretend Gabriel had disobeyed his instruction.

Gabriel shook his head. Old Henry was not going to get the best of him. Not now and not later. Celia's dream wasn't a bad one, not if the war didn't come or if he couldn't figure a way to freedom for a while. Henry would eventually get too old. Then the stables would be Gabriel's domain, and Daniel would be the one running a thrown shoe down to the smithy or walking a sweaty mount cool so it wouldn't founder at the water trough—not breaking his back in the cane fields.

"Come with me, little boy," Gabriel whispered, scooping Daniel up out of his crib box. He began to cry almost instantly. "Grandma Tiley will take care of all that," Gabriel murmured, wrapping his son in his worn jacket and going out into the rain bareheaded.

10

The lightning flashed again, but it was less frequent now, and Celia barely flinched. Madelaine hoped, for Celia's sake, that the storm was passing off to the south.

"Mistress Madelaine?" Hope called softly from the hallway. Startled, Madelaine took in a quick little gulp of air. It was dark now, and the candles burned in their holders on her dressing table.

"Yes?" Madelaine gestured helplessly, too nervous to move. Celia went to open the door.

"Your gentleman is here," Hope announced quietly. Her eyes were twinkling in the light of the candle.

"He is hardly *mine*," Madelaine protested.

"What's he like?" Celia asked, and Madelaine was grateful that she had.

"Very handsome," Hope said. "Can't tell much else yet." Then she raised her eyes to look at Madelaine. "Your mother says to wait fifteen minutes. Come down when you hear the hall clock strike."

Madelaine nodded, feeling the pinch of the corset even more now that her breath was coming a little faster from nervousness. "Tell Maman I will be on time."

Hope gave her a solemn nod, then closed the door again, the click of the latch loud in the quiet of the room.

Celia's eyes were twinkling. "See? Handsome, she says."

Madelaine smiled at her. "You look as if it's Christmas Day."

Celia flashed her wonderful grin, and her eyes shone. "Could be it is. For you."

Madelaine swallowed. "I am so nervous my mouth has gone dry," she admitted.

Celia hurried to the pitcher and brought her a glass of cool water. "Just wet your lips," she cautioned, and Madelaine nodded. The last thing she wanted to add to her nervousness would be to need to run out to the privy. It would be unseemly to return with her hair blown to bits by the wind, but the indoor privy chair was impossible with hoops on.

"Promise you will go right out when the clock strikes?" Madelaine asked Celia, as much to make the time pass as anything else. *Has it even been a full minute yet?*

A flash of lightning lit the room abruptly. The instant it winked out, a crash of thunder boomed close. Celia stiffened like a wooden doll, her eyes wide in fear.

"You should just go home now," Madelaine said.

Celia shook her head, but she held out her hand. They stood together, both of them silent, the minutes crawling past. Finally, the clock sounded downstairs.

Madelaine hugged Celia, then stood straight again and lifted her chin. "How do I look?"

"Beautiful as flowers," Celia said, and Madelaine took as deep a breath as the corset would allow.

"You come with me. Watch from the top of the stairs. The instant I am down and Papa escorts me into the drawing room, you go straight out to the kitchen."

Celia nodded, and Madelaine led the way out the door. Oil lamps were set in niches, each one casting a pool of amber light into the dark hallway. Walking with her head held high, acutely conscious of the way the corset shaped her waist into wandlike narrowness, Madelaine tried to still the pounding of her heart. She passed through the ovals of lantern light, glancing down at the cream lace of her wrap lying on the dark wine-colored silk of her gown. So much preparation, and this man was nothing to her, she scolded herself silently. Not yet, and maybe never, and yet here she was, groomed and shining like a horse at auction.

Celia stopped short of the top of the stairs, and Madelaine nodded to show she understood why. Celia didn't want to be seen. If anyone noticed her, Maman might stop her from leaving. One more glance back at Celia in the shadows, who smiled widely and made a shooing motion with one hand, and Madelaine started down the stairs.

Her father waited at the bottom of the flight, his

arm extended like a beau at a ball. Descending carefully, Madelaine rested her fingertips lightly on his forearm and walked beside him across the landing, then down two more steps into the drawing room. He walked slowly, pacing his usually long stride to her much shorter one, and she was grateful. Between the corset and her heeled shoes, she was a little unsteady.

As Papa guided her through the pillared doorway into the parlor, Madelaine risked a quick look toward the settees in the center of the room. She caught her breath. Rory Quinn was more than handsome. He was an entrancing-looking man with blond hair and striking dark eyes. And the instant he caught her glance, he rose, flashing a warm smile.

Papa presented her formally, and Madelaine curtsied, a tiny motion that acknowledged the formality of the occasion but did not make her look like a schoolgirl, she hoped. "I am most pleased to meet you," she murmured.

Rory's smile widened, then a look of great gravity made it fade. "You cannot be as pleased as I, Miss Madelaine," he said slowly, and she felt her heart flutter, then calm a little. He seemed to like the way she looked. Now, if she could avoid sounding like a ninny, perhaps he would like other things about her.

Françoise stood in the rain-peppered wind. He was a fool. There was no further need to argue the idea with himself. The drawing-room windows were wide enough to see inside, and what he saw only served to infuriate him. Yet he stood here, unable to move, unable to stop staring into the gracious room with its low settees and its enormous hearth. Candles and lanterns were placed about the room, making a twinkling of gold light that accented the beautiful dark furniture.

Madelaine was nowhere to be seen, but Françoise was transfixed, looking at the world she came from, the kind of place she lived in every day. He had never been inside one of the grand plantation houses. Nor had he ever stood so close to one that he could see in its windows before this night.

Françoise shivered against the next blast of wind, wishing he had stayed by the cookfire with the others. This was like looking through a magic glass into another existence. As he watched, Monsieur LeBlanc and his wife, dressed in an elegant gown that prevented her from being able to sit comfortably, were seated on either side of the stranger. Suddenly, Monsieur LeBlanc rose.

Françoise held his breath, waiting. LeBlanc was gone for a full minute, then reappeared in the doorway, Madelaine on his arm. Her gown was even more excessive than her mother's. She was achingly beautiful in it, though, and Françoise could not look away. She was radiant.

Françoise finally forced himself to look up at the sky. Lightning was coming closer, though the rain seemed to be sliding off to the southeast. He wished fiercely that he was home in his father's house, the warm, soft odor of the bousillage walls surrounding him. He thought for one wild moment about taking his *pirogue* from the LeBlanc dock and starting home-ward, then pushed the thought away. None of this should shock him.

"Did you ever think this beautiful girl would have any real interest in you?" he asked himself aloud. "*Non.* So why would you be disappointed when truth proves itself?"

There was no answer to the question that made him feel anything but the fool he was. He looked back through the window in time to see one of the servants come into the parlor, saying something to Madame LeBlanc. She nodded, and they all rose.

Madelaine's dark gown shimmered in the candle-light, but it was her lovely face that made Françoise catch his breath. She was smiling up at the blond man. He was taller than he had looked sitting down.

Celia waited for a long time before she took off her shoes and came forward, barely breathing. She looked down the stairs, knowing she appeared as comically alert as any rabbit passing through the dog yard. She lifted her skirts, her shoes clutched in one hand, and stepped downward onto the first stair, straining her ears. The voices were all far away, from the kitchen or the front rooms, where Rory Quinn was probably los-ing his heart forever, whether he knew it or not yet. The thought made Celia smile.

It would be good when Mistress Madelaine was in love, when she had a baby, too. Gabriel was wrong. It would only bring them closer. And she understood, too, as much as she could. At least she *tried.*

Halfway down, a bolt of lightning seared the sky outside the windows, and Celia shuddered, freezing. When the thunder rolled, shivering the stairs beneath her feet, she pressed her eyes closed and held still, waiting for it to fade, before she could go on. When she opened her eyes, she gasped. Mistress LeBlanc was standing at the foot of the staircase.

"Celia?"

Celia's spine went stiff. "Yes, ma'am."

"What are you doing?"

"Mistress Madelaine said—" Celia began, but Mistress cut her off.

"I don't think help is needed in the kitchen now, Celia. Is that where you were going?" Celia felt a sheen of sweat rise on her forehead. Mistress knew very well that she was terrified of the lightning and thunder. "I was just scared up there," Celia said timidly, "and I—"

"All right, then," Mistress LeBlanc said, smiling blandly. "We have just now gone into the dining room. You may help with service if you can mind your manners. I won't stand for you distracting Madelaine, not even once. Or just help in the kitchen. Being busy will keep your mind off your morbid fear." She put her hands on her hips and clucked her tongue the way a mother would before lecturing a small child. "In all my days, Celia, I have only seen trees struck by lightning. Never a house. You are perfectly safe."

Celia felt her heart stagger, then fall. "But Mistress, I wanted to—"

"I understand, Celia," Mistress LeBlanc interrupted again, and this time there was an irritated expression on her face. "You get scared in storms. Everyone knows that. Now run along to the kitchen. Lily will put you to work at something. Tell her I said to."

Celia nodded numbly, and Mistress LeBlanc turned, her gown rustling across the polished floor. She started toward the dining room, then turned back. "Go on, Celia."

Celia nodded, flinching as a blue-white surge of light blossomed, then winked out, leaving only the amber light of the lanterns and candles behind. The thunder rumbled.

"Shoo!" Mistress LeBlanc chided.

Celia forced herself to come forward, padding down the steps in her stockings.

"And put your shoes on," Mistress LeBlanc scolded.

"Yes'm," Celia said, stopping instantly. She bent her knees to sit on the last step.

"Not *here*, Celia," Mistress LeBlanc said tersely.

Celia swallowed her tears and straightened up just as a rending crash split the sky. She cried out softly.

"Celia!" Mistress LeBlanc said sharply. "This is an important evening for Madelaine. Are you trying to ruin it for her?"

"Oh, no," Celia said instantly, blinking at the tears that burned behind her eyes.

"Then gather your wits and go to the kitchen before she sees you looking pitiful like this."

Celia pulled in a deep breath and started off across

the soft carpets. At the kitchen door, she turned and glanced back. Mistress LeBlanc was just disappearing into the dining room, her steps small and fluid to keep her wide hoops from jouncing like a girl's.

Madelaine sat quietly at the dining table, listening to her father and Rory talking about farming. Rory kept glancing at her, as though he expected her to speak. Madelaine tried to think of some comment to add to the conversation, but she couldn't. Maman was watching her, too, sidelong and carefully, but watching. Madelaine longed to say something provocative, something amusing, but nothing would come to mind.

"Mr. Quinn races horses," Maman said into a small silence.

Madelaine knew this was her cue and only wished she knew half as much about race horses as her mother did. Since she did not, she tried smiling brightly and responding with an inane question. "Is that so, Mr. Quinn?"

He nodded and set down his fork. "I do. It's something I intend to pursue lifelong."

"I love to ride," Madelaine said, and got a look of reproval from her mother. She was supposed to draw out Mr. Quinn's interests, not announce her own. But he seemed interested.

"Really ride?" He grinned. "Or just a stately canter around the park."

"She rides like a sidesaddle jockey," Papa said, and Madelaine was surprised at the pride in his voice. He usually scolded her for being reckless. So did Maman, but now she sat beaming, too, as though she could think of no finer accomplishment her daughter could have.

"Have you ever followed hounds?"

Madelaine tried to meet Mr. Quinn's eyes, but his dark stare seemed to bore through her. She shifted in her chair and blushed. "A few times, yes," she said.

"And did very well," Papa said. "Kept up with the boys her age."

"My brothers taught me to ride," Madelaine said. Then she felt foolish, but Rory leaned forward. He looked so attentive that after a few seconds, she took a breath and managed to tell him about Luc and Alain, where they were studying. "I miss Luc so," she said, then stopped, feeling tears sting at her eyes.

"I am fond of my brothers as well," Rory said. "I taught two of them to ride."

Madelaine hid her tears and listened as Rory began to talk. He described the funniest riding lesson she had ever heard of. His youngest brother had fallen off the horse in every direction. Even the gentle old mare had gotten disgusted with him.

Madelaine's parents both laughed aloud as he spun the tale. She watched him closely and had just begun to relax when he turned his intense gaze on her again and, without interrupting the story, looked deeply into her eyes. Madelaine felt herself leaning toward him, smiling, losing her self-consciousness in the fun of his story. When it was finished, she sat back again, a little embarrassed but grateful that he had taken over and put her at ease. He nodded as though he had understood her thought, then, glancing at Maman and Papa to see that they were looking at each other, he winked.

"And your father is resetting most of the cane?" Monsieur LeBlanc said after a few moments. Rory nodded, then glanced at Madelaine. Her face was polite and attentive again. The elaborate roast her father had sliced so deliberately and placed on her plate had barely been touched. Was she nervous? Because of him? She had certainly come alive when he was telling the story of Edward's first day in the saddle.

"I've had a better time since we changed to burning bagasse," Monsieur LeBlanc was saying. "Using the cane pulp for fuel eliminates much of the woodcutters' toil. I can put the same gangs to work at something else. Roads, usually."

"My father argued that burning the ground-up cane could taint the sugar with an oily taste from the smoke," Rory replied.

"Nonsense!" Monsieur LeBlanc exploded.

Rory had turned his eyes to Madelaine's pretty face. Now he looked back, startled.

"Forgive me," his host was apologizing. "But that is a foul rumor to keep the buyers from dealing with those of us modern enough to try new machinery."

"I meant my father argued that at first," Rory said slowly. "Last year, he bought new machinery himself." Rory looked down at his plate for a long moment, pretending to cut his meat. He really had no interest in this conversation. LeBlanc seemed unable to talk about much besides his farm—at least in the presence of the ladies. Perhaps later, when they were alone with their brandy, he would loosen his tongue a little. Rory wanted his opinions on Lincoln's chances of winning the election, on secession.

Rory would almost be glad when the girl had gone upstairs for the night. He was having a hard time keeping his eyes off her and concentrating on anything else. He was used to pretty women, those he respected and those for whom he bought expensive presents. He was not used to feeling rattled by a woman's beauty.

Letting LeBlanc drone on, Rory looked across the table and caught Madelaine's eye. She was lovely, and the wild night outside the windows proved that her beauty only changed with flashes of piercing light, it did not diminish. Unlike girls who needed candlelight to smooth their skin or put a shine in their hair, this Madelaine was truly beautiful. Nor was she apparently given to the kind of hand fluttering and nonsense that most girls he knew seemed to think attractively feminine. She simply sat with a pleasant expression on her wonderful, clear brow and listened. *A very attractive trait in a girl,* he thought happily.

"And your father is resetting most of his cane?" Monsieur LeBlanc asked again. Rory glanced at Madelaine before settling his gaze on her father's face.

"Yes," he answered, trying hard to look attentive.

"I ground about half of ours early. We finished it up today. I'm using the Cajuns to replant and set seed cane. In another week, I can be rid of them all."

"They have been no trouble, really," Madame

LeBlanc put in. She looked annoyed, but Rory had no time to react.

"Yes, yes," Monsieur LeBlanc was saying. "They have worked out well enough. But extra labor is expensive. Has your father had the same difficulties?"

"We have," Rory agreed cordially, trying to remind LeBlanc that the plantation would be his. "But we have cotton growers close by. They are wiped out, so they're hiring out their slaves at next to nothing."

Monsieur LeBlanc held his glass up for the servant to fill. The man glided forward, poured the water, then stood back again, soundlessly. Rory caught the man's eye and gestured, and he came quickly forward again. Once his glass was full, Rory looked at Monsieur LeBlanc. "Their misfortune becomes our good luck."

"Indeed," Monsieur LeBlanc agreed.

In that instant, a blinding flash of lightning rent the sky. The thunder was deafening and shook the house so that the gaseliers swayed overhead.

"May I be excused for a moment, Maman?" Madelaine asked quietly as the sound began to fade into a rumbling echo.

"Why, dear?" Madame LeBlanc asked mildly. But her eyes were sharp. Rory blinked. This woman was more than she seemed.

"I just wanted to run upstairs a moment," Madelaine said uneasily.

Her mother shook her head. "There is no need."

"But, Maman, I will only be gone a few seconds, and I—"

"There is really no need," Madame LeBlanc said in even, precise tones, looking straight into her daughter's eyes.

"She's worried about Celia," Monsieur LeBlanc told his wife.

"I know," Madame said quietly. "And there is just no need." She raised her chin. "Madelaine has said that she will play the piano for us after dinner."

Rory glanced at Madelaine. Her face was flushed, and her eyes were shining. Her pretty lips were compressed into a straight, stubborn line. There was obviously much more going on here than a simple conversation, but he could not begin to make out what it was.

"She is just worried about Celia," Madame LeBlanc said, addressing her husband and Rory and, seemingly, the rest of the room. She turned her hands palm up as though to share her frustration with her lovely daughter's foolishness. "Her serving girl," she added, shaking her head.

"Celia . . ." Madelaine began, then hesitated and started over. "Celia is terrified of the storms. She weeps the whole time. And trembles," she added, after a quick breath.

"I am telling you, darling girl, there is no reason to worry," Madame interrupted in a pleasant voice that seemed to cover real irritation.

"I will go check on her," Monsieur LeBlanc said, standing up.

"*Non!*" Madelaine gasped, her face a lovely shade of pink.

"I sent her to the kitchen," Madame interjected, watching her daughter's face. "I caught her trying to steal out, Madelaine, but I kept her here."

Madelaine covered her mouth with one hand. "Oh, Maman, *why?* You know how afraid she is."

"I think all of this is taking up entirely too much of Mr. Quinn's visit," Madame LeBlanc said evenly, her eyes fixed on her daughter's.

"I am so sorry," Madelaine said, turning to Rory. There were blush patches high on her cheeks, and she was even prettier than she had been. Rory felt a surge of desire. This young woman was more than he ever could have hoped. What he wanted, more than anything, was to think of some way to get her parents to leave them alone for half an hour. He wanted to talk to her, to find out if her mind could possibly compete with her beauty and her misguided but charming compassion. He would not marry a fool. He wanted intelligent sons.

"I would happily accompany you to the kitchen to see to your servant's welfare," he said aloud. He waited, meeting Monsieur LeBlanc's eyes.

The man merely raised his brows. "Certainly," he said. "Madelaine can show you the way. We will just enjoy the moment of quiet while you are gone."

Madelaine could not believe how accurately Rory had judged her need and how quickly he had solved her dilemma. Rory stood and went to pull back her chair as she rose gratefully, letting the hoops beneath her skirt drop back into order. She smoothed the silk of her gown with her fingers. Rory offered her his arm, and they walked out of the dining room together.

"I do apologize for this," Madelaine whispered as they rounded the corner.

She could smell the soft scent of vanilla on him. He used some kind of fancy shaving soap. Standing this close, his good looks were almost unnerving. He smiled down at her. "For what? I was hoping to find a way to talk to you. I only hope your servant is all right," he added after a few seconds' pause.

"If I tell you something, will you keep it secret?" Madelaine asked. She knew it sounded girlish and silly, but he only smiled and nodded, holding up his right hand as though he were swearing to something in court.

"To my grave." His expression was somber, his gaze very direct.

"I wasn't going up to see to Celia," Madelaine confided, watching his face closely. He moved closer so she could whisper, and the scent of vanilla was spiced with bay. Madelaine swallowed, her mouth dry, feeling her heart speed up at his nearness. "I was pretending to, so Maman wouldn't notice anything out of the ordinary." Rory looked puzzled. She hurried to explain. "I thought Celia was already back at her cabin. I told her to go."

Rory smiled. "So now you really are worried about her."

Madelaine nodded earnestly. "There won't be anyone in the kitchen she can trust."

"You have had this servant girl a long time?" Rory asked.

Madelaine nodded, wondering at the kindness in his voice. Was he an abolitionist? If he did think slavery wrong, he would be the only planter's son she had ever met who thought so. "My whole life. I chose her from all the others when we were both not quite three years old. When she is legally mine, I will free her."

Rory seemed surprised for a second, but then he smiled, and Madelaine hoped he could see how passionately she meant what she had said. Her corset forced her to take shallow breaths that made her breasts rise and fall, and she was acutely aware of his closeness. He released her arm and stepped in front of her to open the kitchen door, then held it while she went in.

Rory watched her without really listening—he had little interest in a serving girl. A dark look crossed her face, then dissolved as she came out of the kitchen, her expression composed. "Will you tell Maman that I will be just a few moments?" she asked. "I don't feel well."

Rory nodded. "Of course. Your servant is all right?"

She nodded instantly. "Oh, yes, Mr. Quinn. Please, just tell Maman I have gone upstairs for a moment. I will be right back down."

Rory smiled reassuringly, hoping she wasn't generally given to the vapors. She didn't look ill. Maybe there was something else afoot, some delicate female matter he would rather not question. He caught at her hand and raised it to his lips. She blushed again, her cheeks flushing like spring roses.

11

❦

The storm had risen slowly, but once it hit, the winds were strong. Françoise huddled close to the wide trunk of one of the oaks that stood at the side of the house. He was staring into the window where Monsieur and Madame LeBlanc still sat, eating in silence. Where had Madelaine and the blond man gone? What was wrong with these parents that they let their daughter walk about the place alone with a man like that?

Françoise turned, disgusted with the LeBlancs, but even more with himself. He was peeking in windows like a boy who longs for love, not a man who has love to offer. He shrugged his shoulders against the buffeting wind, tightening his coat front as he prepared to walk back through the dark to the camp. The campfire would be out by now, everyone huddled in their bedrolls, hoping the storm didn't worsen.

Suddenly, a back door opened, and Françoise saw a

woman come out onto the porch. She was hurrying, her shoulders hunched up, her head down. She was wearing a flat skirt—no hoops—a servant, most likely. As Françoise watched, she hesitated at the edge of the veranda, looking out across the lawns toward the rows of cabins that housed the slaves. She looked miserable, half doubled over, bumping into the column as she stopped at the very edge of the stairs, then hesitated again.

Lightning flickered, and a deep rumble started overhead, rising to a crescendo. The woman bolted forward, running across the grass. The sky lit, lightning running like china cracks across the sky. The woman stumbled and fell. She curled up, then held still, lying faced away from him on the lawn. She was beyond the lights of the house windows now, and Françoise waited for another flash to see if she had gotten up and gone on, just startled by her fall, not hurt.

But when the flash came, the woman had not moved. Françoise ran toward her.

Madelaine hurried up the stairs and turned right down the hall—not left. She had no intention of going to her room. She felt frantic. Celia would be terrified out in the storm alone. Madelaine could not go outside in this weather without ruining her gown, but she had to know that Celia was safely home, not crouched frozen on the grass somewhere.

The storeroom door was sticky, swollen by the damp air, but she got it open on the second try.

Squeezing through, gently angling her oval-shaped hoops through the opening, she managed to make her way between the shelves of household goods. There were bottles of lamp oil and boxes of lye. There was lemon oil for the furniture and stacks of tightly tied bags of cleaning rags that had been torn from ragged coats and jackets, the felt cloth reusable forever in that form. The storeroom was crowded, and for a moment, Madelaine despaired of finding a way through the middle of the stacks of supplies, but she managed. On the far wall, she flung open the door and stood beneath the doorjamb, peering out.

For a long minute, the sky was dark. When lightning crackled on the ink black of the heavens again, Madelaine strained forward to see over the balcony railing, scanning the lawn in the direction Celia would have gone. When she saw her lying like a frightened child, she gasped in dismay. Wildly, she looked around the storeroom, desperate for something that would cover her gown so that she could go outside and bring Celia back safely to her room.

The next bolt of lightning showed Madelaine exactly what she needed, a bedcover, hanging up to air before winter use. Pulling it free of the pegs that held it, Madelaine swung it over her shoulders like an Arab's robe, lifting one edge to hood her hair. Then, without another thought, she ran across the balcony and turned to descend the steep stairs that ended at the far edge of the rose beds. Halfway across the lawn, lightning lit the sky, and Madelaine stumbled to a halt. There was someone else, a man, standing over Celia, pulling at her hand. Madelaine ran closer, her heart easing. If it was Gabriel, she could just apologize to Celia for Maman's cruelty, then run back inside.

But then lightning arced above the house, and the man looked up. His dark hair was plastered to his forehead with rain. *The Cajun!*

"What are you doing here?" he shouted at her.

Madelaine felt a surge of anger at his question as she hurried closer. She lifted her head and pushed her makeshift hood back a little. Then the wind caught it, and she pulled it tight again. "I could ask you the same question," she snapped, reaching down to help Celia to her feet.

"I am so sorry, Mistress Madelaine," Celia whimpered. She was crying, Madelaine saw, but trying hard to control it. "Your *maman* is goin' to have my hide."

"She will be angry at me, not you," Madelaine assured her. For a second, they stood staring at each other, ignoring the man who held Celia's other hand and steadied her with his arm around her shoulders.

"I just wanted to go home," Celia said, looking from the man to Madelaine, then back.

"I will take her out there," the man said evenly. "You go back inside."

Madelaine shook her head. "And why would I trust her to you? You are prowling around my house at night. Why?"

"You are going to ruin your gown and your evening with your beau," the Cajun said sharply.

Madelaine narrowed her eyes. "You were watching?"

If he answered, a gust of wind rattling through the peach trees obscured his voice. The sky laced itself with lightning again. Celia collapsed against his side, and he held her gently upright. "Would you like your father to discover us all?" the Cajun asked Madelaine, almost shouting over the wind. "I will get her home. I give you my word." Then, without warning, quick as a snake, he reached out and grabbed her hand, holding tightly when she tried to pull it free. He kissed her knuckles lightly and let go, brushing her cheek, his fingers barely touching her skin. She glared at him.

"Kind-hearted mistress, go back inside. If your father comes out, you are not the one who will suffer. You know that."

Without another word to Madelaine, he leaned close to Celia and said something to her. She nodded, her face a mask of terror. Then she squeezed Madelaine's hand, looking into her face. "Go on back," she said in a hoarse voice. "He's right about the trouble. Please, Mistress Madelaine, go on home."

Madelaine nodded, and the man smiled at her. "Thank you for taking care of Celia," she managed over the next rattling gust of wind.

The man's smile widened inexplicably, a rakish grin that seemed as eerie as anything else about the night. Lightning crazed the arc of the sky overhead once more, lighting Celia's face and the Cajun's as they stood, side by side, looking at her. Madelaine blinked, seeing something in the man's face she had not seen before. Then the Cajun gestured insistently at her, motioning her back toward the house as he turned Celia about, supporting her weak-kneed walk.

Madelaine stared after them as lightning blinked on, then off again. They went as fast as the Cajun man could manage, and Madelaine watched until the darkness swallowed them. Then she whirled and ran back toward the house, tenting the coverlet over her hair.

He was not just dark-skinned French. *He has mixed blood.* She thought it over and over as she ran back up the steep steps, then under the shelter of the balcony roof. She was puzzled at how upset she was, how agitated. Of what possible consequence to her was a Cajun field worker's ancestry? But as she let herself back into the storeroom and rehung the coverlet, Madelaine's eyes were stinging. First the hurt boy, and now Celia. He had come forward to help people twice—when he could easily have stayed clear of trouble.

Madelaine patted at her hair and face with a clean cotton rag, then arched her back, brushing at a little tuft of grass that clung to her hem. Then she straightened and squeezed her hooped skirt back through the little room and hurried out into the hall, struggling to compose herself.

Gabriel had gotten the first two mares in fairly quickly, without waking Henry. He had seen the old man lying on his cot, eyes closed, mouth open to snore, but he hadn't roused him. Nor would he if he could get away without it. Let him rise to find his neglect covered up and no need to blame anything on anyone. Let him wonder how the mares had appeared safe and sound in the barn. He would know, then, that Gabriel was no fool.

Fingering the lead rope and halter he carried, Gabriel started down the long dark path to the farthest pasture. He smiled in spite of the driving rain. It was good he'd left Daniel with Grandma Tiley. The old woman would make sure he didn't kick his blanket off and take a chill.

The lightning was starting to ease up, Gabriel realized as he had to stop and squint into the dark for almost a minute before another crackling flicker lit his way. Another half hour, and the worst of the storm would likely be over. Except that the wind did seem to be rising. He glanced up at the sky. There were no stars. Maybe it'd just quiet down to a hard rain, then. That would be all right. Just a good heavy rain without more lightning to scare his Celia.

The pasture gate was stuck, swollen with moisture, and it took a minute for Gabriel to force it open. Once inside the fence, he stood still again, waiting for lightning to help him locate the mare. She was likely under a tree somewhere, hunched up against the wind, miserable like the other two had been.

Seconds ticked past. Finally, lightning sparkled to the south, and for a few seconds, the pasture was lit. Gabriel groaned aloud. The mare was under one of the oaks, all right, but she was lying down. That could mean only one thing. He started toward her, wishing he had awakened Henry. The mare jerked her head up and whinnied when she saw him, her eyes outlined in white, her outstretched neck lathered with sweat. Gabriel stopped, then started forward again, unsure what to do. He didn't know anything about helping a colt into the world. But from the looks of the mare, he might not have enough time to get back with Henry to help, anyway.

He knelt at the mare's side, and she rubbed her forehead on his shoulder. He knew that she trusted him completely, just because he had brought her grain and hay for the last few weeks. It made his heart ache when she arched her neck and made a low groaning sound as her sides heaved and tightened.

Celia was so shaky-legged that she could hardly walk. But the Cajun had his arm around her waist, and he kept her moving, faster than she would have believed possible. She closed her eyes against the glaring light that arced above her head every few seconds and let him guide her.

Beneath her terror and the pounding of her heart, she felt foolish and guilty. There would be hell to pay for this some way, somehow, she was sure of it. Madelaine's dress would have spatters on the hem at least. If she was clever enough to hide it, maybe they could get it washed without Mistress LeBlanc finding out, but maybe not, too. It was a long process, and they would have to hang it in plain sight somewhere to get it dry. Maybe they could rub flour into the fabric; sometimes that worked.

"Which way?" the Cajun asked close to her ear.

Celia opened her eyes and was amazed to see the

quarter only a hundred feet ahead of them. "That way." She pointed. "Up toward that end of the row."

The Cajun didn't answer, but he veered, taking her with him, his step firm and steady.

"You married?" he asked after a minute.

Celia nodded, then realized he wasn't looking at her. His eyes were fixed on the uneven, puddled ground they were crossing. "Yes," she told him.

"You will kindly do some quick explaining so he won't want to kill me on sight?"

Celia laughed and felt her fear subside a little, then it surged back as the sky overhead was veined with white.

"Why are you so scared of lightning?" the Cajun asked her, veering again to miss the vegetable garden that ran along in front of the cabins.

Celia hesitated. No one had ever asked her before, not even Madelaine. "I saw it kill a cow."

"Lightning?"

"Dead as dead, and you could smell the meat cooked."

The Cajun didn't answer at first, then he waited for a roll of thunder to subside. "I've heard of that. I've never seen it."

Lightning arced overhead as the Cajun helped Celia up the steps, and she pushed the door open. She took in a quick breath. Gabriel wasn't inside. It was dark, the candles out. She rushed across the room, bumping against the table in the dark. "Oh, my Lord," she said aloud. The crib box was empty.

*   *   *

Rory Quinn rose as Madelaine came back into the room. Her mother stood up, too, and walked to meet her, saying something in a low voice that Rory couldn't hear. Madelaine said something back in a near whisper.

"There you are," Monsieur LeBlanc said as his daughter came forward, walking beside her mother. *They are a handsome pair,* Rory thought. Madame LeBlanc wasn't bad-looking for a mature woman. Maybe her daughter's looks would last past twenty-five, too.

"She says she feels quite ill," Madame LeBlanc said flatly, looking at her husband, then back at her daughter. There was worry in her eyes.

"I am so very sorry to hear that my visit has caused you upset," Rory said smoothly, hoping she would look directly at him. She did.

"Oh, no, it isn't that at all," she assured him. "Perhaps I ate something earlier that I shouldn't have. Or maybe it is the storm."

"Storms never bother you," Madame LeBlanc said. "Don't catch the vapors from Celia, Madelaine."

Madelaine smiled at her mother. "I haven't caught anything, I don't think. I just need to go up and rest."

"Please don't let my presence interfere, my dear girl," Rory said, and he saw her eyes widen a little at his endearment. He smiled even more warmly. "If there is anything I can do to assist you?"

"I will be fine, sir," Madelaine said, and her voice was almost a whisper.

Rory glanced at Monsieur LeBlanc. He looked

amused at the flirting, not angry. He sat up in his chair. "Mr. Quinn will be with us for a few days, I think."

Rory watched Madelaine's eyes widen again and hastened to explain. "Your father has offered to take me around with him on business matters for a little while. I am most eager to learn from his methods. I will inherit Fair Oaks one day, so I like to prepare myself."

Madelaine lowered her eyes again, glancing at her mother.

"Don't let me keep you here, please," Rory repeated. He watched Madelaine glance pleadingly at her mother once more.

"You may go," Madame LeBlanc said. "I will send Lily up to do what Celia should be doing."

Madelaine dropped a tiny curtsy, murmured an apology aimed at no one in particular, and turned around to leave the room.

"You are too hard on her," her father said once she was gone. His wife shot him a stern glance, and Rory knew that she was reminding him that they had a guest in whose presence she would rather not be scolded. Monsieur LeBlanc ignored her. "She is nervous tonight. Understandably. I expect her stomach is upset."

"Yes, dear," Madame LeBlanc said sweetly, and the conversation was ended.

Rory watched them both stare at the paintings on the walls for a moment, then Madame LeBlanc smiled brightly. "My husband tells me that you have a racing mare you are quite eager to prove."

Rory smiled. "I do. She is out in your stable."

"Good!" Madame LeBlanc said. "In the morning, if the storm has passed, we can go have a look at her."

By the time Gabriel was leading the exhausted mare and carrying the dangling-legged foal up the dark path, he had to walk with his head ducked. The wind was not subsiding. If anything, it was worse. The gusts were shoving hard at the trees. He could hear them creaking even over the rushing of the wind itself. He could barely see for the bits of leaves and sand that stung his face when he had to turn straight into the wind to follow the path up the fence line. The foal buried its face in his jacket.

The interior of the stable was ink dark.

"Who's there?"

Gabriel almost smiled. "It's me, Henry," he answered in as even a voice as he could manage. "This last mare dropped her foal. Maybe you can jus' help me get her on inside."

There was a muttered curse, then the pop of a Lucifer match, and the lantern sprang to life.

"You helped her?" Henry said incredulously.

"She didn't need much besides company," Gabriel admitted. "I got the other two caught up easy. This was the only one that took a while."

"You came back," Henry said as he hung the lantern carefully on a nail high above the tinder-dry hay and straw on the floor.

"Thought I'd better," Gabriel answered. Somehow, all the anger had gone out of him. It wasn't just that he was tired, either, Gabriel thought. It was the warm smell of the foal in his arms. It was having watched the colt unfold itself, take its first wobbling step. The wind would have knocked it over if he hadn't been there.

"I liked it," Gabriel said aloud.

Henry nodded brusquely. "There's nothin' like a new foal." Their eyes met. For a few seconds, they just looked at each other. Then Gabriel led the mare forward, heading for the first empty stall.

"Thank you," Henry said from behind him. Then, after a long silence, he said four more words as he forked some hay into the manger. "I'm sorry for this."

Gabriel made a sound of acknowledgment and let it lie. There was no more he needed to hear, really. This was a good night's work after all. He just wanted to get back to his baby boy and his wife before the wind made it impossible.

12

❦

Madelaine could not sleep. The wind was battering at the shutters. After Lily had undressed her and readied her for bed, Maman had come to say that she'd told Charles and Jess to go out and fasten the shutters. They had made quick work of her shutters, then hurried down the balcony to do the next set. Madelaine had pitied them out there in the howling dark.

"And poor Celia," she said aloud, turning from her side onto her back. Her nightdress clung to her skin, and she shifted impatiently to free the soft flannel cloth.

Madelaine felt guilty. Why had she run back in? Was she more afraid of a scolding about water spotting a silk gown than about Celia's safety? The very idea made her ashamed. Why had she taken the Cajun's word? He surely didn't seem like a man who would harm anyone. But why had he been out there in the first place? He had as much as admitted he had been watching through the windows.

∞

Madelaine turned over again, jerking at her night-dress when it tangled around her legs. Sighing, she gave up the pretense of seeking sleep and sat up, throwing the bedding to one side, then stood to light her oil lamp. She began to pace.

Both her heart and her mind felt overfull. Rory had attracted her like no other man ever had. But she couldn't seem to think about him in the dreamy-romantic way she had thought about other men she thought handsome. And she knew why. Her heart was elsewhere.

Why hadn't she ever asked the Cajun man his name? Her father looked down on Cajuns, in spite of Maman's heritage. And most of the white people she knew would be shocked to know she liked a man who had mixed blood. Why? There were scoundrels with faces white as snow and near-saints who lived in the quarter, respected and loved by all who knew them. There were beautiful mulatto women in New Orleans, some of them wealthy and well thought of. And there were white women who walked the docks, dirty and drunk. So what made the difference? Not the color of their skin, that much was sure.

As if to stop her spinning thoughts, the shutters banged, and there was a rending sound so loud that Madelaine flinched. One of the trees? As she stared, her shutters wobbled and strained, then burst open. The wind poured in, rifling through the mementoes on her dressing table, knocking her washstand over. The porcelain washbasin hit the floor and shattered. The oil lamp flickered, but the glass chimney was tall and slender, and it shielded the flame.

Madelaine struggled to cross the room, one hand in front of her face, the wind-driven bits of bark and dirt painful on her cheeks. Leaning out over the sill, she reached to wrestle the shutter closed again. Crying out with effort, she dragged it free of the pressure of the wind and swung it shut. Then, trying desperately to hold it closed, she reached for the other side. The wind wrenched the closed shutter free and slammed it open again. Madelaine tried to grab it, squinting against the raging wind.

"Get inside!"

Bracing herself against her windowsill, Madelaine instinctively turned to look behind herself, thinking that her father or one of the servants had heard her washstand crash to the floor. The quick grasp of a hand on her shoulder made her twist back to face the roaring darkness of the night.

"Get back inside."

Madelaine, blinking against the wind, raised her eyes and saw a faintly lit face, outlined only by her single oil lamp. It was the Cajun man, standing on her balcony.

"Madelaine!" he shouted at her. "Get back inside!" His grip was tight enough to hurt as he pushed her away from the sill. She fought him, startled and unreasoning, twisting to one side. She heard him swear and saw him vault into the room. In one motion, he hooked his arm around her waist and pulled her away from the window, forcing her to stand away, out of the direct line of the gale and flying bits of the wind-torn world that were rushing in the window. "Stay there!" he shouted at her above the roar, and turned away.

Startled, Madelaine lunged to grab at his sleeve, pulling him back toward her. "Is Celia all right?"

The man nodded and leaned close to answer over the shrieking of the wind. "Her husband is home, and their baby and all the mares are safe." Madelaine could only stare at him, grateful, blinking her stinging eyes. Then, inexplicably, he bent and kissed her, a quick, fierce kiss that was over the instant it began. "My name," he told her, speaking so close to her ear that his lips brushed her skin, "is Françoise Jarousseau."

Madelaine stood breathless as he vaulted back outside and closed the shutters one at a time, wrestling them back into place while the wind fought him like a live thing. He did not even glance at her again as he managed to shove them shut. She heard the creaking of the iron catches being cranked back into place, then nothing but the howl of the wind.

Sheldon could feel his wife trembling. He reached out to pat her ample hip and felt how rigid she was, how terrified. He wanted to comfort her, but the truth was, there was no guarantee that the house would withstand a wind like this for very much longer. He was probably as scared as she was.

Sheldon felt the floor planks shake with the next buffet of wind. There were fewer gusts now, just the steady battering that meant this storm was probably a hurricane. He pitied the people down closer to the coast. The sea would probably rise and take whatever it wanted tonight—homes, businesses, and ships. And they would get the bulk of the rain, too, though there would be some falling here later tonight, he was sure. Sheldon fought an urge to open his eyes. It did no good and only made him feel more helpless, dizzier, more trapped. Images of downed cane and ruined fields came into his mind. There was going to be more work than they could manage in a year, even with the Cajuns.

He thought about them, camped past the cut cane on the edge of the swamp. Surely they had sought shelter by now. But where? In the stables, maybe, or one of the storage buildings. Or the sugarhouse itself. He nodded to himself. That was where he'd go. The sugarhouse was brick and stone and cypress timbers heavy enough to stop any wind. Or maybe they had at least made their way down into the creek bottom below the stables.

Françoise could barely breathe. The wind seemed to claw at him, determined to jam his own breath back down into his lungs. It was nearly impossible to walk. He crossed the peach orchard one tree at a time, hanging onto the trunks and resting before he drove himself forward again. Near the edge of the orchard, he stopped and braced himself against a thick-trunked tree. The screaming wind tore at his hair and clothes, and he tried to think.

The wind would not kill him, but it was strong enough now to carry dead limbs and flying debris that might. The best thing was probably to get into a building. He hunched his shoulders, trying to shelter his face from the wind. He knew where the sugarhouse was, and the stables over across the creek, but there were a dozen other buildings large and small scattered over the thousand arpents. In this wind, he was barely able to keep his eyes open. The peach tree he was leaning against shuddered and groaned in the wind. He could feel the wood straining as the wind tried to flatten the whole tree into the earth.

Françoise felt something hit his leg and flinched. He reached down, but whatever it was rushed past, driven by the constant force of the wind. Françoise let the wind shove him across the narrow road. He slammed into one of the old oaks that bordered the lawns and realized he was not far from where he had whistled to get Madelaine's attention while her mother's guests looked at the roses. There would be no roses by morning, he was sure.

Braced against the enormous trunk, Françoise sank to the ground. He had never been out in a hurricane wind like this. At home on his bayou, he would have no more than a hundred paces to walk to find friends or family who would pull him inside to safety and huddle beside him until morning.

He could remember three or four hurricanes when he was a boy, and how Maman had sung in her sweet, low voice, mixing prayer with distraction and comfort until the storm stopped and the sun came through the clouds again. Twice he had seen the hurricane's eye, the calm center of the storm that fooled the unwary into thinking it was over. This was a hurricane, he was pretty sure. That meant the wind would be changing directions at some point, reversing itself. He would have to stay alert enough to move so that the tree still sheltered him when the wind shifted.

Françoise prayed that Philippe and the others were all right. "You should have stayed with them," he said aloud, and his voice was lost in the roar of the wind. He worked his way around the thick trunk of the oak tree and pressed his back up against the rough bark. If he held still, he was in a pocket of slightly calmer air, the force of the storm broken by oak. He was afraid to go any farther. He would pray for the strength of the tree.

And for his life. If this storm did not kill him, Monsieur LeBlanc would.

He had kissed Madelaine. And in the morning, she would tell her father. Then he would be on the run for his life. Monsieur LeBlanc would not take kindly to any man who leaped into his daughter's bedroom in the middle of the night. He would make sure no man ever thought such trespass would be tolerated. Françoise rested his chin on his bent knees and shielded his face with his arms. The instant he could leave, he would. If his own *pirogue* had been blown adrift and gone from the dock, he would have to use someone else's. He shook his head miserably. He was already a fool and a trespasser. Now he was contemplating thievery. And he could do nothing beyond wait for the wind to drop. That could take two hours or two days. The hurricane didn't care. He felt the first drops of rain pelt him from behind and grimaced.

Sometime in the middle of the night, the rain began to fall hard. The steady roar put Celia to sleep at last. When the eerie rose-colored dawn finally came, Celia roused herself and slipped out of bed.

Gabriel had insisted they lie down side by side with Daniel between them. And for hours they had held hands, talking about everything, half the time shouting so the other could hear at all. Then it had gotten too loud to shout above, and they had lain listening to the wind shriek over the top of the chimney, making it whistle like breath over a bottleneck.

It was silent now except for the sound of Gabriel's gentle snoring as she lay curled up around Daniel. Celia tiptoed to the door and lifted the latch. It swung open without sticking, something she could never remember it doing. She blinked, and her eyes stung as the clear light of dawn came into the cabin.

Celia pulled in a long, slow breath, then let it out. This one had been worse than the last. The gardens were raked sideways by the wind, the okra and corn laid flat as though a giant hand had pinned them to the earth. But it was more than that. The ground was littered with live limbs this time. And there was water puddled everywhere.

Celia walked down her crooked steps, staring at the garden. She heard someone cough farther down the row of cabins and turned to see Grandma Tiley standing on her porch.

"All fine?" the old woman called softly.

"Yes," Celia called back to her. Then they both faced outward again, looking at the devastation that would mean starting over, the past month of hard work swept away in a single night by the wind. When Gabriel saw it, he was going to want to weep, but at least he wouldn't be one of the men breaking their backs to get everything in order before the next set of bankers decided to visit.

Celia stretched, looking eastward, hoping the storm was truly past and that this wasn't just the false calm in the center before the wind changed directions. The big house looked all right from where she stood. The shutters were all still closed, but that might be true for hours yet. Master LeBlanc was cautious, and he wouldn't have them opened until he was sure that the storm was gone.

Now, if only the stables were standing and all the stock alive. There were horses that had not been brought in from the pastures, then all the cattle and sheep. It was hard to imagine anything or anyone being able to live through the violence of the night without shelter.

That thought brought a rush of others on its heels, and she peered back inside, looking around wildly. Gabriel had told the Cajun he was welcome to stay. Françoise had lain down on the rag rug in front of the hearth. But he hadn't stayed, obviously. Sometime in the night, he had left. Celia looked back out at the wind-scattered gardens.

"He's gone?" Gabriel asked from the bed.

Celia jumped, startled. "Maybe he went back to that camp they have. He was worried about his friend."

"I'm sorry," Gabriel said tenderly. "I should know you'd be skittish still."

Celia smiled. "You sound like old Henry talkin' about a horse."

Gabriel grinned, and she knew what he was thinking. Maybe that was all settled now. "If the cabins stood, the barns are mos' likely all right," he said quietly.

Celia nodded. The barns had been built of cypress logs as stout as any on the row. They were some of the oldest buildings on the place, made from the huge trees that were cut to clear the swamp when the water was first drained from the fields.

"It looks so different," Celia said quietly. "Worse than the last one."

"Much worse," Gabriel agreed, sliding out of bed, careful not to waken Daniel.

Madelaine woke with a start to a strangely silent morning. She could see the dawn light seeping in around the edges of the shutters, but none of the usual sounds of morning was present. The roosters were silent, and there were no birds singing. From the direction of the quarters, no one was shouting. It was too still.

Getting up quickly and sliding a housedress on over her nightdress, Madelaine opened her door before she remembered what had happened the night before. When she did, she froze in her tracks. He had kissed her. Françoise had kissed her. She raised a hand to her lips and shook her head. Had it been a dream, overly vivid because of the intensity of the storm and her fear? She stepped out into the hall, feeling disoriented and vague, not at all sure what was real and what was not. The Cajun man had helped Celia.

"Françoise," she whispered to herself, looking down the hall. Her parents' door at the other end was still closed. That meant neither of them was up yet. Madelaine hesitated, almost afraid to go look out a window but wanting desperately to see that at least some of her world was still out there.

Madelaine felt her hair brushing the middle of her back on her way down the stairs. She blinked, amazed at herself. She must still be half asleep. Her hair had to be tangled like a bird's nest, and she hadn't even thought to try to brush it out. Celia would do it when she came, but in the meantime . . . Madelaine knew she had better not get caught downstairs. Maman would never approve of her walking through the house in a state of undress and dishevelment where the servants might see her.

Running barefoot across the thick carpets, passing the drawing-room entryway and the hall that led to the wide front door, Madelaine turned toward the kitchen.

It was empty; Lily obviously had slept in. Everything was in its place, the churn set out to dry, the pantry doors closed. But there was a film of grit over everything. Here, on the harder, planked floors, Madelaine could feel it.

She unbarred the door and pulled it open slowly, her heart speeding up as she leaned to look out.

"Is everything all right?"

The voice was concerned and polite and very male.

Madelaine whirled around, conscious of her hair, of the low open throat of her nightdress showing through the unbuttoned bodice of her housedress.

"I forgot you were here," she blurted.

"I have always found hurricanes hard to compete with," he answered easily. Madelaine blushed. After her polished appearance last night, what must he think? But he was smiling, looking at her with a glint of teasing humor in his eyes.

"Is your father up?"

Madelaine shook her head.

Rory grinned. "Well, then, perhaps I won't have to be shot for seeing his beautiful daughter in her night-clothes."

Madelaine tried to laugh as though he had said something amusing, but the truth was, she was completely embarrassed. She had been so busy whispering the name of a Cajun field man that she had forgotten she had had her first proper male caller the night before. What in the world was wrong with her? When her father did arise, she would have to tell him about the Cajun man, about Françoise. Unless it had been a dream. She had wakened a hundred times in the night and dozed fitfully between. Maybe it had been a dream.

"You're still sleepy," Rory said in a teasing tone. "It's unfair to expect you to talk. I have been up for an hour or more. Once the wind dropped, I couldn't sleep at all."

Madelaine nodded. "The quiet is what woke me, too."

Rory took a few steps toward her, then gazed past her, out the door. "Look at that," he murmured, and she turned. She took a quick breath and felt a chill go up her spine. This hurricane had been much worse than the last one, much worse. The poor trees were shattered and broken, their limbs hanging crooked and torn, the yellow-white interior of the wood exposed.

"Who is that?" Rory said from behind her. He was so close she could feel his breath on the nape of her neck.

"Who is . . . ?" she began, then trailed off because her heart was pounding in her temples. He moved closer, resting one hand lightly on her shoulder.

"There, under the trees. A man." He pointed, and Madelaine saw a tall man standing up, swaying on his feet as though dazed.

Françoise! Madelaine thought. He had been out all night in the storm. As she watched, he staggered to one side, putting out a hand to steady himself against the tree.

"Do you know him?" Rory asked. "Or is he some stranger who was blown in by the wind?"

Madelaine stared without answering. So it had not been a dream. He had managed to close the shutters to protect her from the wind after he had gotten Celia home safe. But then the storm had overcome him. He had spent the night without shelter of any kind.

"Madelaine?" Rory asked, reaching to touch her cheek gently. She moved away from his hand.

At that instant, the sound of boot heels clicking on the polished planks upstairs made Madelaine turn. Somehow, Rory was already moving, and by the time her father looked in, he was at a proper distance, just inside the doorway to the kitchen, leaning on the flour bins.

"Good morning," Rory said cordially. "I was just looking for coffee and startled your daughter. Perhaps she was hoping for breakfast." He arched his brows and made a quizzical face as though they had not yet exchanged a word and he was puzzled about why she was walking about in such improper dress himself.

"Close that door, Madelaine," Papa said sternly. "And go upstairs, please, until you are attired for company."

Stealing one last look at Françoise, Madelaine closed the door, then turned and walked quickly out of the kitchen. She could hear Rory's easy laugh as she started up the stairs. He and Papa would spend the day looking over the plantation, she knew, leaving her and Maman to wonder and wait. Celia, at least, would know a little more, since she had to cross the gardens and the lawns to come in to work. And Gabriel would talk to her about the stables and whatever he saw in the fields.

Impatiently, Madelaine flung open her armoire, wishing she could just wear a simple dress without hoops and go outside and see the storm havoc for herself. But she knew her parents would never permit it.

She got her comb and hair box out and sat unhappily at her dressing table staring into the mirror. She looked a fright. *Why in the world did Rory call me beautiful?* Feeling inexplicable tears stinging at the backs of her eyes, she started to work awkwardly at the tangles in her hair. She wanted to go riding today, and she would, even if she had to wait until her father was otherwise preoccupied to tell one of the houseboys to go tell Henry to saddle her gelding. She felt trapped inside, as though there were not enough air in this house for her to breathe.

13

Monsieur LeBlanc sat his horse uneasily. It had been more than a week since the hurricane, and everyone was working dawn to dark—yet the work seemed barely begun. He hated things like this, in disarray, the field slaves spread too thin, levee workers pared down to a minimum.

At least the Cajun crew was working in the north creek field now, planting the seed cane that had been mattressed a few weeks before. The young cane in the field below was still too flooded to work, and it made him sick to look at it, half down and brown-red with mud. Mr. Earley had only two four-man gangs digging drainage ditches. The rest were on the levees. It had rained only one night, but it had come down in torrents. The water was up nearly two feet.

Faint hoofbeats made Monsieur LeBlanc turn in his saddle. Madelaine had been riding every day since the storm, and he wished she would be a little more circumspect about it instead of galloping her gelding up and down the road without proper escort. She ignored his scolding, and he was too busy to watch over her constantly. Her mother seemed equally unable to stop her. It was as though the hurricane had wounded her in some deep way, made her wild and unmanageable.

He had asked her what was wrong, and she had claimed that nothing was bothering her at all. He didn't believe her, but whatever had happened, she refused to talk about it with him or with her mother. He had questioned Celia, too, even though he knew that she would take any punishment before she would tattle on Madelaine. But the servant had looked honestly puzzled when he had asked her and had promised that Madelaine hadn't confided anything in her.

He could only hope that whatever hurt Madelaine during the fear and confusion of the storm would soon heal and that she would notice Rory's obvious interest in her. He shook his head. *How could she not notice it?*

The hoofbeats got louder, and Monsieur LeBlanc saw a familiar sorrel burst into sight, rounding the curve in the orchard road. It wasn't Madelaine. It was Rory Quinn riding toward him at a gallop, running the mare as he did four or five times a day, riding flat-out, leaning forward like a jockey.

Rory was the wonder in all this destruction and chaos. He had stayed, sending word to his father that he was learning too much to leave. And from dawn onward, every single day, Rory had been working like an unpaid overseer, driving the slaves harder than they were used to but accomplishing more in a day than Earley or Sheldon ever had. And he was trying to court Madelaine, too, if she would just stop being so shy.

"Good morning," Rory shouted, reining in his galloping mare as he got close. Monsieur LeBlanc looked at him, envying his youth. Nothing ever seemed to daunt him. There had been ten clear days since the last hurricane, and Rory had made the most of each and every one of them. Monsieur LeBlanc watched as the flighty mare cantered up, breaking back to a trot only when Rory tightened her reins enough to bow her neck. He cut a fine figure, Monsieur LeBlanc could not help thinking. He was going to make a wonderful husband for Madelaine, if she would only stop playing the fool.

"I notice you have fifteen or more arpents worth of ratoons you could plant," Rory called out as he reined in.

Monsieur LeBlanc smiled. This was how the young man started most of his conversations, with a shout. His manners in the parlor were fine enough, but in the fields, he was all business. The mare danced in a circle, and Rory let her, turning his head to keep eye contact. "Where were you going to plant the shoots?"

Monsieur LeBlanc smiled. "I have some marginal land up along the edge of the swamps. I drained most of it last year. I thought I might try and see. Starting from the side shoots is harder than planting seed cane, but the plants seem tougher, at least at first."

Rory was nodding. "My father won't even try it. He

says the lowered juice content makes it impractical, but all the planters down on the delta use ratoons for half their crop or more in years when they are short of seed cane."

"That's what I thought," Monsieur LeBlanc said agreeably. "But we might not get to it now, with all the repair that still needs doing."

Rory nodded. "How are the Cajuns working out?"

Monsieur LeBlanc laughed, shaking his head. "Sheldon has a terrible time with them. He has never overseen free men."

Rory nodded. "My father won't have them on the place."

Monsieur LeBlanc nodded. "I would surely rather not."

Rory pushed his hat back. "With your permission, sir, I will ride out to see if Sheldon needs help. Then I can go back to the sugarhouse."

"I would appreciate it, young man," he said, narrowing his eyes. "You know, I have a colt you might want for all your trouble. He's a beauty, and his dam is the fastest mare I have ever owned."

Rory extended his hand, and they shook, sealing the bargain. "And I will give you back his first colt from a good mare."

Monsieur LeBlanc nodded in assent. This young man had a rare natural grace in every situation. He would be an important man one day. Madelaine could hardly do better.

Françoise kept his head down when Sheldon rode past. He couldn't abide the man and was afraid of that.

Ten days ago, it would not have mattered to him much if he had been run off the place. Now it mattered more than anything. Madelaine rode past the fields two or three times a day now, her hair flying out from beneath her hat, her riding skirt molded against her legs by the wind. And she looked at him when she could. Boldly, meeting his eyes sometimes for five or six seconds as she passed.

He was certain that she was curious about him, that she wanted to stop and to speak. He wished she would. He wanted to apologize to her for kissing her without invitation. He wanted to thank her for not telling her father. She hadn't. It amazed him, but she hadn't.

Françoise had been prepared to run, but that first morning he had been too weak. It was as though every muscle in his body had been exhausted in his all-night duel with the wind. He had staggered back to the place where the camp had been to find nothing there at all. His bedroll, his bag of personal belongings, everything had been gone.

He did not recall lying down or falling asleep, but by the time Philippe and the others had found him and awakened him, it was nearly nightfall. And he knew that whatever her reason, Madelaine had chosen not to tell her father.

"You are humming again," Philippe said from behind him. Françoise turned to grin.

"There is nothing to be happy about," Philippe said soberly. "I have concluded that you are a madman."

"You are the madman," Françoise countered. "You

stopped to gather my things instead of running for your life."

Philippe shook his head. "So you have said before. But I disagree. Perhaps I hoped that you would never return and that a fine bedroll would become mine."

"You would have returned it to my brothers." Françoise laughed.

"Perhaps," Philippe said, looking down at his work again. "We will never know, will we?"

"Is there some problem? Are you men all right up at that end?" Mr. Sheldon called out.

"We are wonderful," Philippe called back in a jovial voice. *"Magnifique!* It is a beautiful day."

"Your insolence will get you in trouble yet," Mr. Sheldon shouted back. His face was red, and he was obviously angry. But somewhere along the line, someone laughed. Almost everyone was bent over, and it was impossible to tell where it had come from. Françoise knew it could have been just about any of them at this point. They were all fed up with Sheldon. And they knew that he would be taken to task now if any of them quit. The second hurricane had changed everything. Once again, the master of the place needed *them* more than they needed him.

"The money is good to have," Philippe said quietly.

Françoise nodded. It was. It would be good to be able to buy some copper hinges and a new plow and perhaps even a young mule to pull it. The way this had all fallen out, he would have money for more than he had ever thought. But the reason he had wanted to fix up his old house had changed. He wasn't thinking about getting a wife anymore. He knew the wife he wanted. And it was entirely impossible that he would ever be able to have her.

Three days later, Madelaine got up at dawn. By the time Celia came in, she was washed up and half dressed on her own, waiting with her corset unlaced. Celia hummed and chattered while she helped. Madelaine was preoccupied, staring into the mirror as Celia curled and brushed her hair. She felt the odd dreamy malaise she had felt every morning since the storm.

"Tell me something, Celia," she said suddenly.

Celia's humming stopped instantly. "Yes, Mistress?"

Madelaine sighed. "How did you know . . . I mean, how could you tell that Gabriel was the one you wanted to marry?"

Celia stood back and looked at her. "I jus' never stop thinking about him. You 'member. You used to scold me."

Madelaine nodded. "You forgot things and walked around in a daydream. And you talked about him every chance you got."

Celia nodded, smiling. "And I was right."

Madelaine turned, and Celia stepped back to look into her face. "Are you happy with him?"

Celia nodded. "Very happy. And with Daniel. There is nothin' like holdin' your very own child."

"I am going to wear riding attire today," Madelaine said suddenly.

Celia tilted her head. "Your mother told me to try to talk you out of ridin' ever' blessed day."

"You can't, Celia. I'll tell her you tried, though."

"Thank you, Mistress Madelaine," Celia said. "I am s'posed to get you to tell me what's wrong, too." She smiled. "What is it?"

"Nothing. Everything. I heard Papa telling Mr. Sheldon that North Carolina would secede if Lincoln gets elected. And that if that happened, Louisiana and the rest of the South would leave the Union, too."

Celia walked to the door, opened it, and looked both ways down the hall, then shut it again. "And that'd mean war?" she asked quietly.

Madelaine nodded, then shrugged. "I think so. No one will tell me anything directly, not even when I ask. But I listen all the time now. And whatever I find out, I will tell you."

"Freedom's too big a hope," Celia murmured, and Madelaine shook her head.

"Maybe not. Lots of people are saying it will come."

"I wish I knew," Celia said, and there was pure agony in her voice. "Not knowin' is worse than anything." Madelaine hugged her, and they clung to each other for a second. Then Celia turned Madelaine back around so that she could finish her hair.

The instant her hat was pinned into place, Madelaine smiled and stood up. "Tell Maman I am upset by not knowing if war is coming," she said impulsively. "Maybe she will tell Papa to tell me what he thinks." Then she led the way out of her room, feverish for the freedom of the gelding's gallop.

As they turned down the stairway, Celia dropped back

a step. It was then that Madelaine noticed her mother at the bottom of the stairs, her face stern. Her hands rested lightly on the silk-draped panniers that topped her hoops, flaring out from her sides like wide, false hips.

"Riding? Again?" she demanded, looking Madelaine up and down. "Madelaine, your father is under enough strain without this nonsense. Since when do you ride every day?"

"You may as well just go on home, Celia," Madelaine murmured. "And thank you very much for helping me this morning."

Madelaine knew that her thanks to Celia would irritate her mother, but she didn't care. Celia flashed her a grateful smile and went past, hurrying through the kitchen door before Maman had time to think of some reason for her to stay. Once through the door, she turned back and smiled.

Madelaine waved, a tiny motion of two fingers that Maman would not notice. She knew that Celia was trying to comfort her. She longed to tell Celia about what was really troubling her heart, about Françoise. But she knew she shouldn't. Françoise had been right that night. If there was trouble, she didn't want it to involve Celia.

"Madelaine!" Maman said in a low voice. "Listen to me."

Madelaine tried to make her face perfectly blank. She tried to erase all the desperation she was feeling so that her mother couldn't see that her heart was aching. How cruel was life, how terrible was fate? She had finally found a man she was drawn to, a man she felt could understand her heart, and he was someone she could never so much as talk to—not if her family found out. It wasn't one thing about him, it was everything. He was Cajun, his blood was mixed, and he was poor, a hired field hand.

"I will come back in before dinnertime," Madelaine said aloud. "I just feel so trapped indoors."

Madelaine stared into her mother's face, afraid to look away from her probing eyes. If she did, Maman would be after her for the rest of the day, trying to find out what she was hiding.

"Something is wrong with you," Maman said. "Has Rory done something, said something . . . ?"

Madelaine shook her head, smiling a false smile. "It's just the storms, Maman. Two hurricanes so close together. It scared me."

Maman lifted her hands in a gesture of helplessness. Her hoops jounced with the abrupt motion. "That is true for us all, daughter. Which is why your father and I need for you to behave as yourself. Not this remote stranger you have become."

"I will try, Maman," Madelaine said softly. Her eyes were stinging, and she knew she was about to cry. The violence and mercurial rise and fall of her emotions confused and frightened her. But she could never tell her mother what was really wrong. "I will be back by dinnertime," she said again, her voice high and brittle-sounding in her own ears.

Maman reached out and tugged her riding hat down over her brow. "Stay covered, or you'll be as brown as a field hand. Rory won't like that."

Madelaine bit at the inside of her cheek but said nothing at all. She was tired of her mother pushing her at Rory. He was handsome, there was no arguing that. And there seemed to be nothing he couldn't do— except genuinely care for another person. She had seen him shouting epithets at the field slaves. He had a way of walking that reminded her of a fighting cock. And sometimes it took him an hour to dress for dinner. The world was a mirror for Rory, and he liked the way he looked reflected in it.

"He is quite interested in you," Maman said.

Madelaine only smiled another false smile and stepped around her mother, her heavy riding skirt billowing out from her legs with every step. Her boots sounded heavy on the planks, like a man's footsteps. Her riding skirt felt unnaturally heavy without hoops beneath to hold the weight of the cloth away from her legs.

Outside, Gabriel stood with her gelding, waiting patiently. When he saw her, he smiled and turned the gelding toward her. Madelaine ran across the lawn.

"Mistress Madelaine," he greeted her. "Good morning." He touched his cap with his fingertips.

"Gabriel, may I ask you something?" Madelaine heard herself asking as he gave her a leg up into her sidesaddle. Gabriel's eyes were flat and unfocused when he glanced up. He still held the reins.

"Yes, Mistress," he said, but she could hear the caution in his voice. She knew she should go no further, and she held her tongue while he fished the stirrup from behind the hem of her skirt and held it as she arranged her legs. He kept his eyes fixed on the horizon, looking past her gelding's head toward the peach orchard. Madelaine stared at the side of his face as she settled her skirts, and he handed her the reins. He really was a very handsome man, tall and broad-shouldered. It was easy to see why Celia had been drawn to him. *But is that love?*

"What makes you love Celia?" Madelaine asked impulsively.

Gabriel glanced at her sidelong, and she could tell that the question had startled him.

"What makes me . . . ?" he repeated.

"Why do you love her?" Madelaine repeated. "I want to understand about love."

He shook his head. "Mistress Madelaine, that's a question for your mother."

"My mother is not a man," Madelaine said sadly. "My father would never tell me, and my brothers are in Paris. There's no one else I *can* ask."

"There's no why to it," he said finally. "I jus' do."

"You sound like you are sorry about it," Madelaine teased him, hoping he would say a little more, but he only frowned as he let the reins loose and stepped back. "You have a good ride now, Mistress Madelaine." He hesitated, then pulled in a deep breath. "I am s'posed to tell you to watch out for the mud bogs up 'long the cane field road."

"I never go up there," Madelaine said incredulously, staring at him. "Who in the world told you that?"

Gabriel looked down at the dirt. "Jus' you look out up there. Don't gallop. Ride the woods path slow."

Then, before she could say another word, Gabriel was walking away fast, his hands in his pockets.

14

Celia was waiting at the stable when Gabriel got back. "I brought you some pastry pie," she said when he frowned at her.

"I know why you're here," he groused, taking the cloth-wrapped bundle from her hands. "You want to know if I tol' her."

She smiled at him, looking around. "Grandma Tiley has Daniel, but I got to get back quick; she's bakin' pies in the big house today. They want somethin' special for that Rory." She looked pleased with herself, like a little girl with a secret. "He struts like a rooster. I can tell Mistress Madelaine doesn't much like him now."

Gabriel held up a finger. "Celia, hush."

"Henry is up at the pasture," she told him. "I saw him walk off when I came up. Did you tell her?"

Gabriel grunted, relaxing a little. "I did."

Celia smiled and kissed the end of his nose. "She asked me how I knew I loved you."

He shook his head, his stomach tight. Messing in the affairs of white people always led to sorrow one way or another. A horse inside the barn whinnied.

"Don't you care to know what I told her?" Celia asked, and tilted her head. She looked beautiful, and he could not help but smile a little.

"I tol' her you were so pitiful I had to take care of you, or no one ever would." Celia teased him, then laughed softly when he frowned. "I tol' her the truth. That you make me happy."

"She asked me why I loved you," Gabriel countered.

Celia's brows arched like a cat's back, and he had to smile at how startled she looked. "She didn't!" Celia breathed.

He nodded. "She did. But I tol' her to ask her mama questions like that, not me."

Celia's eyes shone. "She mus' be in love with him! That's why she wants to know."

Gabriel frowned again, glancing up as another horse whinnied inside the barn. "It'll be nothin' but trouble if it is so."

Celia nodded, but her eyes were still dancing with a girlish excitement. "Mistress Madelaine's in love! And I like him, don't you?" she said in a singsong. Then her face sobered. "You're right, though, it'll be nothin' but trouble for us all. Master and Mistress are never goin' to allow it."

Gabriel spat into the dirt. "White people never do things by themselves. They have to get us all wound up in it. Your precious Madelaine is goin' to get us both hurt with all this."

Celia shrugged, and her face clouded. He saw the last little bit of dance go out of her eyes. He was sorry to take it from her, but he knew he was right. "She's waltzin' around dazed just now," Celia said. "But she wouldn't do anythin' to hurt us. And she—"

A sound inside the barn made Gabriel reach out, covering Celia's lips with his hand. An instant later, Rory Quinn came ambling out the big double doors, emerging from the dim interior.

"Good mornin'," Gabriel called, shooting a fierce glance at Celia. "I'd have saddled the mare, sir, if I knowned you wanted her."

Rory looked at them, narrowing his eyes. Gabriel felt his heart slow, then speed up. How much had the man heard? He glanced at Celia again. She looked scared. What exactly had they said?

"Your mistress go riding again this morning?"

Celia nodded without speaking.

"Yes, sir," Gabriel said, his voice level as though nothing were wrong.

"Do you happen to know which way she went?"

Gabriel felt his heart hitch again. He shook his head. "She would never tell me anything like that, Master Quinn. But her mother might know." Quinn nodded brusquely and swung up into his saddle.

Françoise waited in the woods. Every rustle in the leaves, every bird call, made him turn and stare down the path. When he finally heard hoofbeats, he ran his hand through his hair, afraid it would be the blond man, or Monsieur LeBlanc, or even Sheldon using the

173

back road for some coincidental reason. It wasn't that he had no fear of what they would do to him if they found him with Madelaine. It was just that as real as he knew the danger was, his need to see her was stronger than any fear he could feel for himself. It didn't matter what they did to him.

"Or what they try to do to me," he said, letting his anger override his caution as he stepped out to stand just behind an oak that overhung the path. He could see from here, looking straight down the path a half mile or so. The hoofbeats were louder now, the rider was galloping hard. Whoever it was, the rider was alone.

"You could die for this," Françoise said aloud, but he didn't move into deeper cover as the horse came closer. They would have to catch him first, and he was, after all, a Cajun standing at the edge of a swamp. They knew nothing about his world. They didn't know where he lived. Philippe would never tell them, even if they thought to ask him. And none of the rest knew exactly.

The first glimpse of the galloping bay made Françoise catch his breath. She had come! A few seconds later, entering the far end of the woods, she pulled her mount back to a prancing trot. She was peering into the trees, her head high, her hat pushed back on her forehead so that she could see better. He waited until she got close enough so that he could see the lovely rose pink of her cheeks and lips. Then he whistled, a high, silvery melody, and saw her smile, twisting in the saddle, scanning the line of trees at the edge of the road until she saw him. Then she urged her horse toward him. He caught the reins to stop her, and she leaned to let him lift her down out of the saddle.

Madelaine was breathless with excitement. Françoise helped her to the ground, and they stood staring at each other.

"I didn't think you would come," he said finally.

She nodded, entranced by the color of his eyes. They were like the sea, changing with the light. "I am not sure why I did."

"I know this is impossible," he said, and his voice held such sorrow that her heart ached.

"You kissed me that night," she said, without knowing that she was going to.

He smiled. "I did. I am sorry."

Madelaine regarded him. He was handsome in a way she couldn't describe, even to herself. His dark hair and sea-green eyes were wonderful, but it was more than that. His eyes were direct. That's what she had noticed about him the first time she had seen him. She reached out and touched the soft homespun cloth of his shirt. She had never worn cloth like it, simple and strong. He touched her hand, then lowered his own.

"Sophie, my sister-in-law, wove the cloth," Françoise said. "I thought the wind had taken this shirt from me last time. But Philippe saved it for me."

Madelaine loved the musical lilt of his accent.

"Philippe?" she asked, just to keep him talking. He drew her to one side and led the way back into the cover of the woods.

"He is a neighbor of mine. Like a brother."

"Do you have brothers and sisters?" Madelaine could feel her legs trembling. He didn't scare her, it wasn't that. She felt as though something inside her had been set free. She could feel it; he didn't expect her to be amusing or clever or accomplished. He only wanted to know who she was.

"Three brothers," he answered. "No girls. Which is a shame. But Antoine, the eldest of us, now has a daughter with all my *maman's* beauty and kindness. She will be a *traiteur*, I think, like Maman."

"A *traiteur?*" Madelaine echoed.

He nodded. "A healer. Maman was very good. People came from far and near for her help."

Madelaine remembered the hurt boy, and she was about to ask him about what he had done, but he smiled. "And you? Brothers and sisters?"

"I have two brothers," Madelaine said. "They are studying in Europe."

Françoise nodded gravely, waiting for her to go on. She found herself talking about Luc. About how they were closer than anyone else in the family.

"Antoine is like that with me," Françoise said when she was finished. "But he advises me whether or not I ask. Sometimes it makes me angry."

Madelaine nodded. "Luc thinks he knows all about the world . . ." She trailed off, laughing.

"You had better go back," Françoise said abruptly.

Madelaine felt a pressure in her chest, but she nodded. Of course, he was right. She wondered if he would kiss her again. She wanted him to. But he only helped her back onto her gelding, then stood a moment holding the reins, gazing into her eyes. "Will you come again?" he asked, exhaling and glancing aside.

"I will," she promised.

"Then I have a reason to wake up in the morning," he said, his face perfectly serious. He turned. "I will wait here until you are well away," he said.

She nodded, but it took a moment for Madelaine to turn her gelding back toward the road.

Rory wasn't quite sure why he had followed Madelaine. He had heard snippets and bits of the talk between the house servant and the stableman, though he had not caught much beyond Madelaine's name and something about explaining love to her. It was the slaves' reaction when he had come out of the stable that had set him thinking. They had both looked startled and uneasy.

More than that, the woman had looked familiar. Rory was pretty sure it was the housemaid who always waited on Madelaine, though he wasn't positive. He had never really looked at her closely as she hurried upstairs or down, attending to her duties. And he hadn't wanted to ask. The housemaid might tell Madelaine he had questioned her.

All Rory's life, girls had simpered and giggled when he turned his attention on them. He was the eldest son of a wealthy man, and he knew very well he was handsome. Madelaine was a beauty, but she was an innocent girl, and instead of swooning, she had suddenly become immune to his advances, treating him politely but without much interest. And it had begun that morning after the hurricane. Something had happened. He meant to find out what.

Following the fresh set of hoofprints that led up the road toward the cane fields, Rory let his mare canter. It was easy. There had been a spattering rain in the night that blurred all but this morning's tracks, and Madelaine was riding at her usual mad gallop, her gelding leaving deep hoofprints and flung earth down the center of the road.

Rory let his mare have her head until he spotted Madelaine in the distance. Then he slowed immediately, hauling back on the mare's already taut reins. Madelaine's gelding had been chosen for steadiness and good temper, not for speed.

When Madelaine turned off the main road and headed west, Rory was puzzled. It was dangerous to ride so close to the swampland, even this time of year when the cooler nights kept the snakes torpid and sleepy this early in the morning. When she slowed her gelding, he reined in, too. When he saw the tall man emerge from the trees to lift her from her horse, he jerked his mare to a plunging halt, astonished.

Rory pulled the mare hard to the side, riding into the trees. He swung out of the saddle and tied the mare, then made his way forward on foot. Finally, through the trees, he could see them. They were standing awkwardly, ten or fifteen feet apart, talking. So, it wasn't as bad as he had thought. But this was the very beginning of a dalliance that would cost

Madelaine everything if he allowed her to pursue it. This man was obviously unsuitable. Rory couldn't see his face, but his clothes were cheap and worn, and he was bareheaded like a Cajun. The idea of some rough-mannered field hand touching Madelaine's delicate skin made Rory physically sick. He watched them a few seconds more, then ran back to his mare. Once mounted, he reined her around hard enough to make her rear.

This was foolish. If he rode in like an avenging angel and gave the scoundrel what he deserved, Madelaine, in the way of all romantic young girls, would swoon with despair and a broken heart. It would only make her more attached to this man, who-ever he was. Rory did not want Madelaine to hate him. He wanted her to melt under his touch. The truth was, he wanted to marry her.

Rory pulled his mare around in another circle, star-tled by the sound of hoofbeats. She was leaving this soon? Then perhaps what he had overheard had noth-ing to do with this. Perhaps it was a chance meeting, and he had misinterpreted the man's gesture in help-ing Madelaine down. They had been standing a proper distance apart, and they had only been talking.

Rory forced his mare into a thick stand of willows, taking his chances that there wouldn't be a snake. In seconds, Madelaine rode past, her head high, her expression remote and dreamy.

Rory stayed hidden, waiting. A few minutes later, a tall, lanky Cajun walked past, whistling. The tone of his whistle was extraordinary. It was a high, clear melody, as pure as a silver flute. As the sound hung in the still morning air, Rory had to restrain himself from leaping from the bushes and beating the man senseless for his audacity in compromising Madelaine's propriety.

Instead, he fixed the man's mixed-blood face in his mind. Perhaps he was infatuated, but he would respect Madelaine's honor and her eventual rebuff. Or perhaps not. It really didn't matter. Honorable or not, he would soon have to be dealt with.

The plantation bell was ringing. Riding back after the dinner break, Sheldon glanced up at the sky. Still clear. If they got another few weeks without rain or heavy frost, they would be all right. He refused to hurry. The Cajuns would still be straggling back down from that swamp camp of theirs, anyway. He'd had to ride up there the week before and had been amazed at the work the men had put in after a day in the cane. They'd redug fire pits and latrines, and they had shelters rigged up out of palmetto woven as fine as any hatmaker could do. They'd dug a pit for roasting something big, he saw. He should probably tell Monsieur LeBlanc to make sure the sheep and the pigs were counted every evening.

This week, they were setting ratoon shoots, thick and short with roots hanging down like fibrous wire. The field had been plowed into furrows about six inches deep. The Cajuns used broad-bladed hoes to bed them in, pushing the soil inward to cover them.

As Sheldon got closer to the field they were working, he noticed that the Cajuns had fanned themselves out from one end to the other again. This wasn't a new trick. They did it whenever he wasn't there to stop them. This was the practice at their *coup du main* parties, one of them had told him. Each man took a certain number of rows, then worked at his own speed. What he didn't finish today, he would catch tomorrow. It made the field a ragged, uneven patchwork that no one but the damn Cajuns could figure out.

Sheldon resented it. If one man quit or decided to stop in the middle of a row, only someone walking every inch of the field would be able to tell. And if there were unplanted gaps in the rows, he would be the one answering to Monsieur LeBlanc about it next spring.

Idly, Sheldon counted heads. *Thirty?* He blinked. This morning, there had been twenty-nine. "Was someone sick this morning?" he called out.

A few of the men looked up and stared at him a few seconds before looking back down at their work. None responded to the question. Somewhere on the far side of the field, one of the men began to whistle a high, clear melody. Two or three others joined in, and one man cut a figure, dancing as though he had a woman in his arms. They all laughed, then went back to work. Sheldon spat in the dirt, disgusted. He didn't understand the joke, but he was sure he was the butt of it somehow. *Cajuns.*

15

❧

Three days later, there were clouds to the south. Monsieur LeBlanc could not stop watching them, glancing in that direction every few minutes as he and Rory rode side by side along the levee.

"It's a fine morning," Monsieur LeBlanc said by way of breaking the silence.

"Yes, it is," Rory agreed. "How are the Cajuns working this morning? I haven't been out that way yet."

Monsieur LeBlanc gestured. "Sheldon says another day, and we will be done with them."

"Consider keeping them on another week," Rory said.

Monsieur LeBlanc narrowed his eyes. "Why?"

"Because you ought to let them do the repair work inside the granaries. Let them make that mud plaster they are so good with."

Monsieur LeBlanc leaned forward. "I wanted to let the Cajuns go. I have field hands who know how to do it well enough—"

"None so well as the Cajuns, sir," Rory interrupted him. "They work miracles with their *bousillage*. Let your field slaves plant the lower field with ratoons before frost. Then, if weather holds next year, you'll make up the loss from this one."

Monsieur LeBlanc shook his head. "I haven't considered planting beyond the fields I had already planned." He frowned. "But you have a point."

"It's a gamble, but not a big one," Rory said. "And if frost holds off, it will pay off handsomely."

"We have to finish grinding what the wind has knocked down as soon as we can and—"

"All the more reason to keep the Cajuns on. Mattress what's left in case it frosts, then divide the slaves between planting and the sugarhouse."

Monsieur LeBlanc shrugged, conceding the sense in what Rory was saying. For the twentieth time, he wondered when he had stopped being young and reckless—when he had gotten so afraid to take risks that he never even thought of them anymore. "It depends," he said aloud, "on whether the Cajuns can be talked into staying. Sheldon says they are ready to leave."

"Sheldon hates them. He'd rather they did," Rory said, and Monsieur LeBlanc joined him in quiet laughter. Sheldon rarely opened his mouth lately except to complain about the Cajuns. It was clear he resented Rory overseeing the field crews and wanted his old job back.

Monsieur LeBlanc looked back out across the fields. "I suppose they want the wages. Most of them are earning more money than they have seen in their lives all at once."

Rory nodded. "They grumble, but they'll stay on if you offer them another week's work."

Monsieur LeBlanc glanced up at the sky. The nights were getting chilly. If he was going to gamble, it was now, or forget it. But the truth was, he was tired of having the Cajuns around. The tall, lanky one who had talked to Madelaine was seen now and then over at the quarters. Madelaine said he had done Celia some favor and that he and Gabriel got on well—that he was visiting, nothing more. But the whole idea of his slaves befriending a Cajun made Monsieur LeBlanc uneasy. He would put a stop to it if it went on.

"Just for another week or so?" he said aloud. "You think they can repair the granary in that amount of time?"

Rory made a quick cutting gesture with his right hand. "No more than that. Then you will have this place ready for winter with no more work left than splitting up the downed wood they are piling in the orchard now."

"That much sounds good," Monsieur LeBlanc admitted.

"And I will oversee one or the other. If Sheldon is tired of Cajuns, I can take a turn."

"Your father is probably missing your help," Monsieur LeBlanc said.

Rory laughed. "He will send for me if he needs me, I assure you."

Monsieur LeBlanc nodded, this time decisively. "Well, I will not offend you by offering to pay you, but I would like to give you something besides that colt."

Rory's smile widened. "Well, if I am lucky and persistent, perhaps you will, sir, perhaps you will."

Monsieur LeBlanc laughed with Rory, understanding him perfectly and liking him even more for his tact in not mentioning Madelaine's name aloud.

The days passed like water running in a clear stream, bright and quick. Every time Madelaine rode to the woods, Françoise kissed her again, then held her back, staring into her eyes so long she felt as if he were looking into her soul. He was careful not to let her stay too long, not to let anything happen that should not happen between them like this, hiding in the woods. He loved her, he said. He would suffer any hurt before knowingly hurting her.

Sometimes they talked. Other times, they held hands and could not manage to talk at all, only to touch and, more and more often, to kiss.

"Are you all right?" Françoise asked the moment she dismounted, sliding from the saddle into his arms.

She leaned against him. "Yes. As much as I can be."

"I will take you to a *fais do-do* one day," Françoise murmured, breathing the sweet scent of her hair, astonished at the words that were coming out of his mouth. But he could not seem to stop them. "We will dance until dawn, and our babies will sleep in the loft room until the music stops."

Madelaine did not pull away. She put her arms around him. "I want to live like that. I want to have babies and dance and laugh and—"

"And work hard?" Françoise asked, afraid of her

answer. "I will never be a rich man. I will need your help every day of our lives."

Madelaine's lovely face flushed. "I hate all the hours I spend doing nothing. I hate all the time my mother spends making me walk properly and sit properly. And eat and talk and laugh and—"

Françoise laughed aloud. "You sound like an angry little girl."

Madelaine pouted, her lower lip sticking out. Then she smiled. "But you can't imagine what it is like not to have anything useful to do all day. Nothing that matters, I mean. Nothing that makes any difference to anyone."

Françoise studied her face, imagining her helping his brothers' wives as they wove and dyed their cloth. He pictured her in a striped skirt without the massive ruffles and elaborate design that made each one so hard to wash and iron that only the work of slaves could keep her wardrobe in order. If the war came, if the slaves were freed, all this would change. The sugar planters' lives would be turned upside down. He wondered if she knew that—had ever thought about all that it took to keep her house spotless and polished and her clothing in perfect order.

"You're right," he whispered. "I cannot imagine. Kiss me again, my love."

She rose on her tiptoes and kissed him, a girlish brush of her lips as usual. But then she held him harder, and he found himself responding, kissing her for a long, sensuous moment. He stepped back, holding her at arm's length. "Your father would whip me for that. And he would shoot me for my thoughts."

Her eyes flooded. "How can we . . ." She trailed off.

Françoise tried to smile at her. "Perhaps if we talk to him, together. You have told me about him, that he is a reasonable man, a good man."

Madelaine looked at him. "Oh, Françoise . . ." She leaned toward him, but he sidestepped. It was nearly impossible not to sweep her up into his arms and carry her off somewhere where no one would find them, no one could stop them from promising each other their hearts and lives. But she would hate him for that one day, and that day would not be long in coming. If her parents disowned her, her beloved brothers condemned her, how long would she love him? The idea of her hating him was more than Françoise could bear.

"You need to leave," he said.

Madelaine dabbed at her eyes and sniffled. "But we will find some way to see each other again soon?"

Françoise nodded. "I will ask Gabriel to carry the messages as he has been. We don't have long. Another week, since I am going to help with the *bousillage* plastering. But after that . . ." He trailed off because he had no idea what to say to her. He had been lying awake every night, trying to think of a way to approach her father. He was afraid Monsieur LeBlanc would set the dogs on him before he even got close to the front door.

Madelaine leaned against him again, and he let her, his thoughts spiraling as he held her close.

Françoise kept hoping that Rory would leave, but the man seemed to be making himself at home here at Belle Grove, and it was obvious that Monsieur LeBlanc liked him a great deal. Françoise exhaled, not wanting to bring up Rory's name with Madelaine. If she gave her life ten minutes' practical thought, she might very well decide to marry the man. Idleness and ease were easy to denounce before they were left behind.

Françoise kissed the top of Madelaine's head, holding her close. How much longer could either one of them stand this? "You must leave now. Someone will notice."

She shook her head. "Papa and Rory were out on the levee, talking. I came quietly and slowly this time, just as you said."

Françoise squeezed her shoulders, then forced himself to step back. "I want to marry you." He watched her face closely, and, to his joy, he saw her eyes light up, widen. She nodded, smiling. There was no hesitation, no shadow of doubt.

"But Madelaine," he added, "we can't deceive your father like this for long. It is even more dangerous for you than for me."

Madelaine nodded again. She looked miserable, and he knew exactly what she was thinking.

"I know," he said quietly. "Your parents will never allow it. Nevertheless, it is what I want."

"It's what I want, too," Madelaine said evenly, looking into his eyes.

Françoise tried to see into her heart, into her soul. She was so young and so sheltered. "Hard work and small farm. That is all I have to offer you. And love."

"And a reason to wake up in the mornings," she whispered.

"There are dances," he told her, watching her face.

"The people of my family and others gather and work all day to build a barn or to harvest the corn or some other big chore that takes many hands. Then we dance and celebrate, and the children play outside while we eat and sing . . ." He trailed off, waiting for her to talk about some grand ball her parents had given, but she didn't. She nodded gravely.

"Maman has told me stories of her grandparents all my life. They lived in the swamp. I went to their house once, when I was a little girl. I loved it there. It was a small, clean house with a stairway outside that led up to—"

"The *garconiere*, where the sons had slept as boys," he finished for her.

"I remember the girls most of all," she went on, "running through the yard, those beautiful colors, not a single one tripping over hoops. They climbed trees! I couldn't. I remember all of them laughing." She looked so beautiful, her eyes intense as though she was willing him to believe that she knew enough about his life to want it, too.

The faint sound of hoofbeats made them jerk apart. Wordlessly, he boosted her back onto her horse, then watched as she rode parallel to the road for some distance and cautiously guided her horse out into the open. She looked both ways, then waved at him to let him know it was all right. Whomever they had heard, it had been far away. She reached up to set her hat and looked back at him. Then she galloped away.

The next day, Celia was working in her garden. Daniel was asleep, and Mistress Madelaine was practicing her piano. It was hours before supper, and it was wonderful to have a little time to clean up her patch of vegetables. Grandma Tiley's stretch of the long garden was always immaculate. So was Trudy's on the other side. Only her own looked as if no one loved it enough to pick up a hoe.

"Sssssst!"

Celia whirled around, nearly dropping the hoe. She scanned the edge of the peach orchard, expecting to see Trudy on her way back from milking cows. But no one was there. What had the noise been, then?

You are imagining things because you are worried, she scolded herself, and set back to work. The garden was nearly dead for the year, but she wanted to get the weeds out of the seedrows anyway. It would be harder when the weather warmed up with the stalks dry and brittle. And she would gather them up and burn them, which would kill at least some of the seeds.

"Ssssst!"

Celia stood up slowly this time, acting as though she were just rubbing her back. She looked into the orchard again, shading her eyes with her free hand. "Françoise?" she called softly. "Is that you?" There was no answer, no further sound at all. It made her uneasy for the rest of the week.

As always, Madelaine galloped the last stretch of road. These meetings had become the most real part of her life. With Françoise, she felt free to speak her mind, to say what she thought. He didn't hush her or remind her to be ladylike when she used angry words about slavery or said she was afraid of the war coming. He told her what he knew, what he thought.

"*Bonjour*, beautiful girl," he said, swinging her down out of the saddle and kissing her gently.

Madelaine stood on her tiptoes to kiss him a second time. Then she linked her arm though his, and they walked back into the cover of the trees.

They had found a spot, well off the road, where an old oak had been cut, the broad stump providing a roughhewn bench where they could sit and talk. He allowed her an hour, afraid to steal more time, afraid they would be discovered. She was grateful that he was so careful and concerned about her reputation. If it had been up to her, the whole day could have flown past before she thought about leaving his side.

"How is Rory?" he asked, and she saw the glint in his eye when he spoke the name.

"Maman and Papa are fond of him, you know that. I find him offensive." She smiled. "And you know that, too."

"He is dangerous," Françoise said quietly. "Please do not anger him. Philippe says he knows someone who described Rory as one of the nightriders who beat old Lanille within an inch of his life."

Madelaine held very still while Françoise recounted the incident and what his brother had said about it. "They are riding less often," he finished, "or so people are saying. Perhaps they are all too busy rebuilding their farms. I just wish he would go back to his own place. Surely that will be soon?"

Madelaine leaned against his shoulder. "What will

we do?" she asked, knowing that he would understand her perfectly.

Françoise was silent for a long time. Then he sighed. "It is not a question of what we will do," he said finally. "It is a question of what your father will do."

Madelaine closed her eyes, knowing he was right.

Late in the afternoon, Gabriel was walking the mare with the newest foal in the upper pasture. The colt bounded in circles around its dam, spindly legs working furiously, its neck extended.

"Halloo!"

Gabriel turned, startled. Master Quinn was leaning on the gate. "Yes, sir?"

"Nice-looking colt. Bring him over here, would you?"

Gabriel turned the mare toward the gate, and her colt followed, sticking closer now, made wary by the presence of a stranger. Rory climbed the gate and dropped to the ground. He patted the mare, moving slowly along her flank. Then, abruptly, he lunged forward and grabbed the colt. The little horse squealed and struggled, his eyes circled in terrified white. The mare flattened her ears, angling her back feet toward Rory.

"Hold her still!" Rory commanded.

Gabriel tried, but the mare was frantic, wheeling around to strike out with one foreleg.

Rory jumped clear, dragging the colt with him. The mare's strike hit the colt in his back leg, just above the hock. He squealed again and arched his back like a fish, freeing himself from Rory's grip. He ran four or five strides before he stumbled to a stop and stood, holding his right back hoof a few inches from the ground.

"What in hell are you doing?" Rory shouted, his face flushed.

"I couldn't hol' her, sir," Gabriel said slowly, considering the best way to react. He could not get angry, of course, he could not give in to his desire to punch this white man's face as hard as the mare had wanted to strike him. The colt was wobbling, limping forward, a little steadier than he had been a moment before.

"Are you new to the stables?" Rory demanded, dusting his trousers.

Gabriel hesitated, then nodded. "I was tryin' to tell you, sir. But you were jus' too quick for me."

To Gabriel's huge relief, the man smiled, looking flattered. "You have to be quick to get hold of the little ones like that." He glanced at the colt, and Gabriel followed his gaze. The colt was still favoring the leg, but it looked as if it was going to be all right. Nothing broken, no tendons torn. Gabriel looked back at the white man. "I am surely sorry, Master Quinn."

"I thought I saw that tall Cajun up at your cabin the other day," Rory said matter-of-factly, and the change of subject caught Gabriel so off guard that he couldn't react at all. He stared at Quinn, trying to read his intent.

"He's a friend of yours, isn't he?"

Gabriel hesitated again. "I only know him from

him workin' here, Master Quinn. I don't know anything about him from anywhere else. He helped my missus one day."

Quinn narrowed his eyes. "Helped her what? You had better keep an eye on your woman, Gabriel."

Gabriel's anger blossomed into rage. He kept it off his face and out of his voice. "I will do that, Master Quinn."

Rory looked out over the pasture, glanced at the colt, then stared into Gabriel's eyes with an intensity that was unnerving. "You'd better not have anything else to do with him, you hear me? He's only going to cause trouble for you and for—what's your wife's name? She's the one who likes to garden, isn't she?"

"Celia," Gabriel murmured.

"Quit doing him favors. Both of you."

Gabriel tried to make his face blank, but he knew he hadn't concealed his reaction well enough when Quinn laughed. "I don' do him no favors, sir," he said aloud, trying to repair the damage.

Rory stopped laughing. "Make it true, Gabriel. Just make that true from now on."

He turned on his heel and walked back the gate, vaulting over it like a boy of fifteen. Gabriel watched him go, then turned to tend the colt, his heart and stomach tight with fear.

Early the next morning, Madelaine was waltzing, alone, humming the orchestra's melody, imagining her father and Françoise standing side by side in black suits, their top hats off and under their arms. Spinning to her imaginary vision, she whirled, her light housedress swirling with her, the silk whispering against her hoops.

"Mistress Madelaine?"

It was Celia's voice from the hallway. Breathless, Madelaine ran to her door and flung it open. She leaned out to glance up and down the hall before she spoke. "Do you have a message?"

Celia shook her head, half turning to look behind herself. "Gabriel says we can't do it no more."

Madelaine felt her heart skip a beat. "But . . . Celia?" She was close to tears. She pulled Celia into her room and closed the door. She went to sit at her dressing table, and Celia automatically followed her and picked up her hairbrush. This had almost become a habit. If Madame LeBlanc opened the door unexpectedly, they would not look like conspirators.

"I am jus' so sorry, Mistress Madelaine," Celia said quietly.

Madelaine could not answer for a long moment. Then she drew in a shuddering breath and nodded, meeting Celia's eyes in the mirror. "I understand. I do."

"Gabriel said you'd be angry at us, but—"

"I'm not angry, Celia," Madelaine interrupted her. "I'm just . . . oh, Celia, I love him. Can't you understand that? I—"

"Gabriel says it's better if I don't ever talk to you about all this," Celia interrupted, her voice soft and sad.

Madelaine could only nod. She had known all along that she and Françoise should not have involved either Celia or Gabriel in arranging their meetings, but there hadn't been another way. "What will I do?" she asked Celia, turning to look up at her.

Celia shook her head. "I don' know. If you run off with him, your father and the nightriders will jus' find you and—"

"Nightriders?" Madelaine repeated. "Papa has nothing to do with those men. He would never . . ." She trailed off, standing up to look directly into Celia's face. "Does he?"

"And Rory and Master Sheldon, Gabriel says. He can tell. Their horses are sweated out and rough next morning. It's when there's a moon to ride by."

Madelaine felt physically ill, remembering all the bits and pieces of stories she had heard. "The hangings?" she whispered.

"Your father was here that night, 'member? He was sick."

Madelaine felt a weight go off her chest. Of course, that was right. But Rory hadn't been. And Sheldon? Pudgy little Sheldon a vigilante? Françoise had told her about the Cajun man who had been beaten, about Antoine's belief that his mixed blood had been the cause.

"Gabriel heard Master Rory braggin' 'bout it to Master Sheldon one day. Kind of hiding what he was saying, you know, but not good enough."

Madelaine sat back down, her knees suddenly weak. She couldn't live with knowing these things. She couldn't live *here*.

16

❧

Rory walked around the stable once more, thinking the plan through, searching it for holes. There weren't any that he could see. It was dark out, still early. He hadn't done anything to conceal his presence. If old Henry was awake, he was certainly not alert enough to notice someone prowling about. Rory kicked at a rock, then scuffed his boots along the ground. There was no stir from within. It was entirely dark, not a hint of candlelight from the open double doors or from the unglazed window in the tack room.

Rory almost laughed aloud. This was going to be so easy, it would barely take an hour out of tomorrow night's sleep. He picked up a pebble and tossed it against the side of the building. He heard a faint sound it took him a few seconds to recognize. Old Henry was snoring. The two times he had come and gotten his mare for night rides, the old man had awakened and offered to help, then gone back to sleep when told he wasn't needed. Gabriel, of course, didn't sleep here. He was with his wife in their cabin.

For an instant, Rory let himself consider changing his plan, switching to the cabin as a target for the fire. In a way, it made more sense. The Cajun might have gotten angry at his friends for refusing to carry his messages anymore. Rory assumed it was his talk with Gabriel that had stopped the meetings. He had kept a close watch on Françoise and the man had been at work early and had not left until just at dark with the others. Madelaine had retreated inside herself these past few days, too, her demeanor remote and unhappy. She was pining for her Cajun, he was sure. So it was time to prove to her that the man she was infatuated with was not worthy of her.

Rory tossed one more pebble. It struck the stable wall and rattled downward. Again, there was no response from within. Perfect. Two or three more days, then, no more than that. He would trick Françoise into a fight if he could, or at least make him angry enough that people would believe he had started the fire. It was going to be very simple. The nightriders would take care of everything, and he wouldn't have to do any more than go along with them to catch the arsonist. LeBlanc wouldn't mind Judge Lynch presiding over this trial, he was sure. And Madelaine would be safely his, her reputation intact.

The sun was getting low in the sky, and Françoise was glad. It had been a very long, very unpleasant day. He missed Madelaine fiercely. It was torture to think that he might never see her again. But Gabriel had explained, and there was no denying he was right.

At the sound of hoofbeats, Françoise glared sidelong at Rory Quinn. The man was insufferable today, shouting orders, riding back and forth. And why? This was the last day of work. At least he had left them alone for about an hour before their dinner break, disappearing without an explanation. Françoise had hoped that Sheldon would be the one to oversee them for the afternoon, but they'd had no such luck. Quinn had come galloping up just as they'd all finished eating.

Françoise looked back down at his work. He was helping the others shred the moss, chopping at it with short, measured strokes. Long, uncut strands were worked into the clay, too. There was no shortage of *barbe espagnol* here. It was so seldom used that the swamp was full of trees draped with the hanging curtains of silvery moss.

Philippe and three others had dug the mud pit days before, and it had been filled and emptied many times since then. Belle Grove had its own clay blank, just as it had everything else, or so it seemed to Françoise. These plantation men had little need ever to talk to their neighbors. How different was the life they led compared to his own. Could Madelaine ever have been happy living with him? Perhaps not. But it was wrong that it was not her choice, that she couldn't love him if that was where her heart led her.

"Stay awake, Françoise!"

The shout startled Françoise, and he jerked around

to see Rory Quinn glaring down at him. Françoise narrowed his eyes. He had never told the man his name.

"You're holding them up!"

Françoise looked back to see the carriers unloading moss from the next cart. He stepped back, getting out of their way, using his hoe to rake the loose moss toward himself. The others in the line had already done so. The instant he was clear, the carriers dumped fresh moss in a windrow in front of him and the other men who were chopping.

"If you can't keep up the pace, quit now and go home, Françoise," Quinn said, too loudly. There was a snarling quality to his voice, and Françoise stared at him. Did he know? How could he? Celia and Gabriel would never have told. Françoise was sure of that. They would keep it a secret for him, but far more to protect themselves and Celia's beloved Madelaine.

"Here's the clay," Quinn shouted, announcing what every man with his own eyes open could easily see. Françoise felt his fists tighten. Quinn had been like this since they had begun, abusing them, screaming at them to do what they were already doing. But he had never singled Françoise out before this.

The clay wagon rolled up, the mule trotting under old Henry's whip. Quinn had insisted Henry drive the mule, even though any one of them could have done it as well. Henry looked exhausted. The day was hot in spite of the season, and there was a rim of clouds to the south. It was humid, everyone sweating and red-faced.

Françoise squinted at the clouds. They were moving

this way. The weather couldn't hold forever. It would have to rain soon, and then the levee would need every spare man, and the roads would need dredging every day, and firewood would need cutting. Françoise found himself wondering if he could somehow stay on at Belle Grove, a hired hand. Which would be worse, to see her from afar or never to see her again?

The mule came to a halt, and two men began unloading the heavy clay with narrow-bladed shovels, pitching it into the mud pit. Water was added from the barrels that had been filled from the little fishpond above the sugarhouse. Then the moss line got moving, and Françoise took his turn, carrying all he could, leaving his short-handled hoe beside the fresh moss.

The *bousillage* they were making was of middling quality, no more, Françoise knew. No one cared enough to make it truly fine. Had it been a neighbor's chimney or a friend's walls, they all would have worked much harder, tearing the moss by hand instead of chopping it with the hoes.

Françoise dropped his armload by the pit, adding to the pile that was already there, then he turned to go back to his place beside the fresh moss. Others were carrying long strands down from the moss wagon. Those would be added more slowly, each one worked into the mud before another was put in. There was no oyster shell here to burn. Without the black ash from oyster shell, no *bousillage* could be truly strong.

"Françoise?"

He looked up. Rory Quinn was gesturing at him. Françoise glanced back at Philippe, who shrugged at him, then stooped to pick up his hoe. He held it high, like a weapon, his eyes fixed on Quinn, his meaning clear. Françoise stepped out of line and crossed the granary yard, looking up at Quinn, who sat his horse straight and tall.

"I've been thinking," Quinn said.

Françoise met his eyes but didn't answer.

"I want you to pack up your things and leave. Now."

"We were to finish the granary," Françoise said as evenly as he could, trying to figure out what Quinn might be trying to do, and why.

"You're getting in the other men's way. You aren't keeping up."

Françoise frowned.

Quinn's face was calm, reasonable. "I think you had better do as I say, Françoise."

"We have never been introduced, sir," Françoise said politely and coldly. "My name is Monsieur Jarousseau."

"Not to me, it isn't," Quinn said in a voice so low no one else could hear. "And I want you out of my sight. Go back to that pigsty of a camp if you like, but leave before nightfall."

"Monsieur LeBlanc is the one who hired me—" Françoise began.

"But I am letting you go," Quinn said in the same low voice. "Now. Get off this plantation now, or I'll have you whipped. Go home. Whatever wages you are owed I'll send with your big friend." He gestured vaguely toward Philippe, who still held the hoe ready.

Françoise knew he was half an instant from dragging the man off his horse. Then a single thought stopped him. Even if Quinn knew, he might not have said anything to Madelaine's father—because he wanted her for himself, and he wanted her with an unsullied reputation. But men blurted things out in a rage. If he provoked Quinn now, the man might only make things worse for Madelaine. Much worse.

Françoise laid down his hoe, then turned around and walked away. Philippe stared at him, and Françoise made a smoothing motion with one hand. There was no point in arguing. "I am going home. He says you can bring my wage," Françoise called out, and Philippe nodded, glancing back at Quinn. Françoise didn't. He refused to.

Celia held Daniel tightly as Gabriel paced, repeating what Henry had told him he'd seen. "I just don't think Quinn is going to let Françoise go without doing something."

"But what?" Celia patted Daniel's back, glancing outside. The clouds that had been hanging in the south were coming closer. And there was a stiff breeze picking up. There were no leaves left on any of the trees after the first two hurricanes, but those that had fallen were skittering on the worn dirt between the cabins and the wide lawn.

"I don't know," Gabriel admitted after a long silence. "How is she?"

Celia smiled at him, grateful. She knew he didn't care about Madelaine any more than he did any other white person, but he asked because he knew she cared.

"Her heart is jus' plain broken," Celia said. "She cries when no one is looking. The res' of the time, she looks ill. She won't talk to me 'bout it. She says it ain't fair to get me in trouble."

Gabriel nodded, hoping it was true, that Mistress Madelaine would not yet manage to pull Celia into the middle of something terrible.

"I hope it don't storm tonight, at least," Celia said. "Or maybe Françoise is already home."

"Quinn," Gabriel spat, saying the hated name without the white man's title of "Master" in front of it. He heard Celia's little sound of concern and knew she had understood his thoughts perfectly. "I hate them all," he said, and saw her face tighten. "I do," he said. "If that war comes, I will fight them with my own hands if I can."

"And Daniel will jus' grow up without a father," Celia whispered.

Gabriel reached out to hold her, sorry he had upset her more than she already was. Daniel, pressed between his mother's soft breasts and his father's familiar chest, gurgled happily. Gabriel smiled, and Celia exhaled slowly. If Françoise could just get away, and if Mistress Madelaine's poor broken heart would only heal, the world would be back to rights.

"When do you go back up to the big house?" Gabriel asked, breathing close to her ear. He kissed her neck.

"Now," she told him.

He released her and kissed the tip of her nose. "Well, the minute you can, you come on back to me."

Celia nodded, smiling at him, trying not to let her worries over Mistress Madelaine cloud her eyes.

Rory had found the lamp oil in the upstairs store-room nearly a week before. All he had done this night was to wait for dark, then take three bottles of the thick, smelly stuff and put them in a bag with four or five packets of Lucifer matches. The bag was home-spun cottonade that he had taken from the Cajun camp. There had been twenty just like it, used for all manner of things.

Henry would be as soundly asleep as he had ever been this night, Rory had seen to that. The old man had managed to work out the day but had left looking dog-tired. Even the rising wind would work in Rory's favor, setting the cow and hay sheds behind the stable afire quickly. He would raise the alarm from the house, spotting the flames from his balcony, and the fire would be put out before anyone was hurt. The Cajun's sack would be found, with the matches in it. He had already mentioned his difficulty with Françoise to Monsieur LeBlanc and why he had let him go. Monsieur LeBlanc had understood and approved.

Rory had considered taking his mare out of the sta-ble for the night, but it would have looked odd, and there was really no danger. The wind wasn't blowing all that hard. And if the fire did spread, he would be close enough to get the mare to safety. The creek was close. The buckets would be easily filled and carried. The plan was foolproof.

And, of course, the Cajun's sack would be found on the far side, as though Françoise had dropped it running away. Rory had decided that the lamp oil bottles would go back in the storeroom, empty. If anyone else noticed oil had been used to start the fire, it would be Celia who would fall under suspicion, not him. After all, she was Françoise's friend.

Because Madelaine loved the servant girl, Rory decided not to implicate her by leaving the bottles in the sack. But if the bottles were noticed, well, that would only be worse for the Cajun. It was known that Françoise had come to Celia's cabin many times to visit. A man who incited slaves to criminality was regarded as far more dangerous than a murderer. If the missing oil were discovered, things would go hard for Françoise when the nightriders caught up with him.

Rory began to hum nervously, opening the first bottle of lamp oil. The trick would be not to use too much. He didn't want the fire to burn more than the cow sheds. The wind kicked up, rattling leaves along the ground. Rory ignored it. Everything was set up perfectly, and he didn't intend to lose this opportunity to settle the matter of the Cajun once and for all.

With luck, Madelaine would be frightened, and he would be able to comfort her. Her recent silence at dinner had started to grate on his nerves. Her excuses when her mother suggested they picnic in the orchard or go riding together were becoming tedious.

Rory wanted her to start looking to him for protection instead of her father. Thinking about Madelaine clinging to him, scared and flushed with excitement, Rory poured a little of the oil on the ground. He struck a Lucifer match, and the blue-orange flame sputtered to life. He managed to shield it from the wind, but the flame surged when it touched the oil, then winked out. Patiently, he poured more oil, this time soaking the foundation log. He had plenty of matches, and plenty of time.

17

❧

Françoise could not sleep, and the night refused to pass. He wished a hundred times he had just gone when Quinn had ordered him to. But Philippe had talked him into staying out of sight until morning, then leaving with the rest, afraid that he'd come to some harm alone, either in the storm or because someone followed him. He argued that Quinn was the kind of man who would hire revenge or even fabricate some story to tell the local nightriders, and Françoise knew he was right.

Françoise shifted in his bedroll. Antoine had been right, though not in the way he'd thought. The plantation men were dangerous. And Philippe had been right about the storm. The rising wind sifted into his blankets and his uneasy thoughts. Staring up into the moonless darkness, he tried to make himself accept that he would never see Madelaine again, but it was impossible.

Once he was sure the others were asleep, Françoise rose quietly and walked away from the camp, the stiff wind buffeting him, giving him something to fight. Without thinking about where he was going, he began to walk toward the pillared mansion that held Madelaine prisoner. The wind was getting stronger by the minute, and overhead there were winks and flashes of lightning. It was a thunderstorm rolling in, at best. At worst, it would be another hurricane. Françoise shook his head. That was hardly possible. No one had ever heard of there being three of the monstrous storms so close together in a single season.

On the road that led down through the orchards, Françoise chided himself. This was useless. He would not even see her. They would have the windows shuttered against the wind by now, or very soon. And if he did glimpse her in the drawing room or sweeping down the hall in one of her elaborate gowns, what good would it do?

Françoise's thoughts were interrupted by a distant sound of commotion, carried on the wind. He cocked his head, then faced sideways so that the sound of the wind rushing past his own ears was dimmed. Yes. It was voices, and more than one, he was pretty sure. It was hard to tell over the howl of the wind.

Knowing it was smarter to stay out of any trouble that might be brewing, he began to walk toward the sound. He heard hoofbeats and stepped out of the road just in time for a horse to gallop past, so close that its shoulder grazed his lightly.

Stumbling, turning to look as a flicker of lightning

lit the sky, Françoise thought he recognized Mr. Sheldon but wasn't sure. The rider, whoever he was, did not rein in or look back. Françoise turned and kept going. He had nothing to lose, really. In the morning, he would be leaving the only girl he had ever loved, forever. He couldn't make himself care about much else.

Mistress Madelaine was out of her evening clothes and wore only her loosened corset and chemise beneath her housedress. It had no hoops, and she was sitting on the edge of the bed, swinging her feet back and forth like a girl. "And Rory made him leave?" It was hard to hear her over the sound of the blustery wind outside, and Celia had to lean closer. "Why, Celia? Why would Rory do that?"

Celia heard the anguish in Madelaine's voice and wished she had fibbed when Madelaine had asked if there was any news of Françoise. "He jus' ran him off the work crew," she said aloud. "Henry couldn't much hear what he said."

Madelaine was biting at her lower lip, her eyes shiny with tears. "And now he is gone forever, and there is nothing I can do."

Celia murmured a soothing response. There was nothing to say. Gabriel was right. They had all known from the beginning that Madelaine's family would never allow her to be courted by someone like Françoise. "I should never have talked Gabriel into carrying the messages," she said miserably.

Madelaine stood up. Outside, the wind rushed past

the window, and a half instant of flickering light made Celia's stomach tighten. *Oh, Lord, no . . . not a thunderstorm,* she prayed silently. *Not tonight on top of everything else.*

"These damn storms," Madelaine said, and Celia took in a quick breath. She had never heard Mistress Madelaine curse before in her whole life. The oil lamp on the dresser was smoking, and she stood to trim the wick, glancing out the window.

The odd ruddy light off toward the stables confused her for a moment, then she realized what she was seeing. "Fire!" she said, but her voice caught, and it seemed to her nothing came out. Still, Madelaine must have heard, because she jumped up, looked out the window, then gasped and turned, running for the door, stopping only to scoop up the lamp on the dresser to light their way. Celia followed. Madame LeBlanc was coming up the stairs.

"Your father is already down at the stables," she said evenly to Madelaine. "He says we are to stay here, inside the house, unless he tells us differently."

"But Maman—" Madelaine began.

"We will do as he said," Maman interrupted her sharply, then looked past her. "Celia?"

Celia came forward a step. "Yes, Mistress?"

"Master LeBlanc and Rory have ridden to the fire. Sheldon is riding for the Cajun camp, and Mr. Earley is organizing the field hands. You are to run out and waken everyone in the quarter."

"Yes'm," Celia said from behind Madelaine. Her knees felt like calf's-foot jelly, trembly and weak.

Madelaine held the lamp to one side and embraced her quickly, then released her and faced her mother.

"Let me go, too. I can help Celia, Maman. She is afraid of the storm, and—"

"You will obey your father!" Mistress LeBlanc said in a high, brittle voice. She held her candle high, turning. "Celia, don't waste another second!"

Celia lifted her skirt above her ankles and ran for the stairs.

Pounding down the orchard road in the dark, fighting the wind-blown dust, Monsieur LeBlanc could only be grateful that Rory Quinn had been awake and pacing his balcony. If he had not spotted the fire, there would have been no chance at all to stop it. There was little enough now. They would need every man they could muster, he was sure. The wind was rising by the second.

Rory Quinn had been remarkably calm, staying behind a few seconds, instructing two of the servants to get the storm shutters fastened and three others to find and carry every bucket on the place to the stables. Earley and Sheldon had been sent for and instructed.

Monsieur LeBlanc ran as fast as he could, his shirt-tails flapping out behind him. The wind was fierce, and he could only pray that what he feared wasn't true, that this storm was not another hurricane. And worst of all, if that was the case, it seemed so far like a nearly dry one. This was one night when they desperately needed rain to help them stop the fire, and the sooner the better.

Rounding the last corner, Monsieur LeBlanc cursed beneath his breath. He could see the flames. The stables weren't on fire yet, but the whole row of cow sheds was, and the flames were creeping along the ground, nearly flattened by each gust of wind, then springing back up. Interlaced with the salty ocean scent of the wind was the sharp smell of smoke. Monsieur LeBlanc began to shout.

The slaves were just standing and staring at the flames. Trying to organize them into action, Monsieur LeBlanc realized Rory Quinn was nowhere to be seen. After a few seconds, Mr. Earley rode up, his mare wild-eyed and dangerous. He turned her into the cow pen and then helped Monsieur LeBlanc, screaming at the slaves to line up and get themselves ready to pass buckets from the creek up the slope.

"Madelaine!" Maman said angrily.

Madelaine focused on her mother's face. "Let me go help Celia."

Maman shook her head. "The last thing I need is insolence from you. Now, get dressed and come down to the kitchen as quickly as you can." She pivoted and went back down the stairs.

Madelaine didn't want to dress. She absolutely dreaded sitting in the kitchen next to her mother, wringing their hands and worrying. Doing nothing of any use. Struggling against a sense of desperation, Madelaine went back up the hallway. She slowed, then stopped before the door of her room, but she could not make herself go in.

After a few seconds, she held the lamp high and continued down the hall, heading for the storeroom door. She could at least watch to make sure that Celia made it safely to the cabins. Closing the door behind herself, she realized it would be much easier this time, without big hoops. Madelaine set her lamp on a shelf, then tried to open the door. She couldn't. The wind had pinned it shut, resisting all her strength as she pushed on it with both hands, then braced her shoulder and heaved.

In the darkness of the crowded little room, Madelaine stood back, feeling breathless and helpless. Then she heard the storeroom door rattle as though someone were turning the doorknob. She gasped. Maman would be furious with her if she were discovered here.

Madelaine leaned to blow out her lamp, then clapped her hand over the top of the glass chimney to contain the acrid puff of smoke that would rise from the wick. She stepped back, positioning herself at the end of the shelves, behind her mother's dress forms.

The door opened, and the amber light of a lamp came into the storeroom. Madelaine pressed herself against the wall, her heart hammering. But it was not her mother who came in, or Hope or Lily. It was Rory Quinn. He was breathing like a winded horse, carrying three bottles of lamp oil. His face shining with sweat, he reached up, setting the bottles on the shelf. Then he turned and went out. She did not hear his footsteps on the planks. *He's trying to be quiet? Why?*

After a long moment standing in the dark,

Madelaine took a Lucifer match from her housedress pocket and relit her lamp. She held it at eye level, moving down the line of shelves. There. Three of the bottles were nearly empty. Madelaine reached up. There was an inch-long twig stuck to one of them where the glass had gotten oily. Madelaine looked at it carefully, recognizing the deep red color of the wood instantly. It was a peach twig.

Gabriel struggled out of a deep sleep, wrenching over on his side and striking out at the fists that were pounding at his side. "What? What!"

"Gabriel! There's a fire!"

Celia's voice was sharp. He opened his eyes onto darkness, then blinked and saw that she had lit their lamp and set it behind herself on their little table. The light made a shadow of her silhouette as big as the wall, grotesque and slanting as though she stood on a different floor from the bed.

"Fire!" she repeated.

Gabriel sat up.

"Fire down at the stables. Help me wake everyone!" She shouted above the wind, and he realized how much worse it had gotten while he slept.

Gabriel shoved the covers back. "You start at that end." He pointed toward Trudy's cabin, then pulled on his trousers, hopping on one foot to keep his balance.

"Leave Daniel here?" Celia shouted.

He nodded. "Only jus' long enough to get folks up, then come back for him. Don't leave him a second more 'n that. The wind is still comin' this way. I'll go straight on to the barn to help Henry."

He said no more, and he didn't need to; Celia understood him perfectly. They were downwind from the stables. If the fire swept this way, Daniel would be in danger.

"Go on!" Gabriel shouted at her, and she realized she was staring at their son. Amazingly, he still slept soundly. She gathered her skirt and whirled for the door.

Madelaine had gone back into her room after Rory left the storeroom, but she had stood by the shutters instead of dressing, staring out at the distant half globe of reddish light from the fire. She thought about her gelding, with his handsome face and willing spirit. She thought about old Henry running in his ragged, lopsided way, trying to coax panicked horses to safety. Gabriel would soon be there to help, along with all the others. And all the Cajuns. Would they help? Even though Rory had insulted Françoise?

Madelaine dug her nails into her palms as lightning streaked the sky above the red light of the fire. Where was the rain? The two hurricanes before this one had brought drenching rains, flooding rains. The way the wind was rising, this was another one. *Dear God, why should this one be dry?*

Madelaine knew she should dress, should join her mother, who was no doubt sitting alone in the kitchen. For an instant, Madelaine felt something as wild and relentless as the wind rising inside her heart. She should get dressed properly, then go down to Maman. That was what she should do, what she would be expected to have done when all this was over. Worry and wait. That is what her father had said she was to do. But she knew she couldn't. Never again. She was finished with sitting by while other people did what mattered.

Madelaine buttoned the front of her housedress and reached for a shawl. She would not put on hoops or tighten her corset. Not now. She said a prayer for Françoise, that he was home, safe, in the shelter of the house he had told her about with such pride and happiness in his eyes. She wanted to tell him that she loved him. She knew it was true now and regretted not saying it. If she could get a message to him through his friend, he could come back, and they could run away together.

From the wind-filled world beyond her window, Madelaine heard raised voices and the sound of ladders thudding against the side of the house. Then she heard a sharp banging off to the right of her little balcony. In minutes, Jess and Charles would come up the stairs and fasten her shutters closed from the outside. She could not open the storeroom door, and she would never sneak past Maman downstairs. This was her only chance.

Madelaine opened her window, climbed over the sill, and stepped out onto her balcony, turning to close the sash behind her. The wind slammed against her as she stepped away from the side of the house, instantly tearing her hair free of its pins. She could hear Jess and

Charles more clearly now, arguing about something, shouting to hear each other over the wind. They were at the base of the balcony stairs, coming up.

Madelaine clenched her fists. She could not see them yet, so they couldn't see her. There was no light from stars or moon, only the dark howl of the hurricane. It wouldn't be long before the wind would be strong enough to kill. She swung her leg up over the rail.

Thankful that she had not replaced her corset or put on hoops, Madelaine started down the trellis backward. Without reasoning with herself about where she was going or why, she clung to the thick tangle of honeysuckle vine, her whole body shaking. When her feet finally touched the ground, she turned and ran across the lawn in her kidskin house slippers, expecting every second to hear Jess or Charles shout at her. But they didn't.

When she stopped beyond the rose gardens, slowing because it was too dark to run through the limb-strewn orchard, she heard snatches of their voices again, still arguing about which shutters to close first. They hadn't even noticed her. She faced the living current of the wind, heading for the stables, not at all sure what she meant to do when she got there. Lightning crackled overhead, arcing like silver veins across the sky. But there was still no rain.

Françoise saw the cow sheds ablaze and ran the last stretch of the orchard road, the wind assaulting him from behind as he came around the bend. He took off his jacket to wet it in the creek. Then he struggled over a corral fence and stood wide-legged against the force of the gale, beating at the flames.

There was a commotion up on the road, and he could hear shouts and curses in a dozen voices. Lightning showed him slaves standing in a loose knot, with Monsieur LeBlanc screaming at them, gesturing wildly. Then the sky went dark, and Françoise went back to work, slashing his jacket at the flames, hearing wind-splintered voices as the men organized themselves into a bucket brigade.

A flash of lightning split the sky overhead and spread out in a branching arc that flickered, lighting the whole scene for ten or fifteen seconds. Françoise looked up and saw a man standing on the road, staring at him. It was Rory Quinn. Before Françoise had time to react, the sky went black again. Unsure why he was doing it, his instincts awakened by the intensity of Quinn's expression of surprise, Françoise backed away from the ruddy light of the flames and made his way toward the shadowy peach orchard. His jacket was nearly dry from the heat of the fire, and he put it back on.

Celia shifted her weight from one foot to the other, standing on her narrow planked porch, watching as the last of the men disappeared, heading for the stables. They each carried two buckets or three, however many they had around their cabins. Gabriel had thought to tell them. She would have forgotten.

The wind tore at her hair, and she tightened her scarf just as lightning spread overhead like brilliant silver roots of some midnight tree, appearing, then disappearing to leave the sky black again. She said a prayer for rain to start soon.

Daniel was stirring. Celia went in, shutting the door tightly behind herself. She picked her baby up, comforted by his warmth, and nursed him back to sleep. Once he was settled in his crib box, Celia found herself glancing at the door, even though she knew that Gabriel would not be coming home for hours and hours. She paced back and forth, ignoring the flashes of lightning. The wind was so loud that the thunder was almost erased.

Grandma Tiley would be alone in her cabin, Celia thought suddenly. She gathered up Daniel and his blankets and held him tightly against her chest as she went out the door, shoving it hard to open it. Fastening it awkwardly behind her, she ran close to the front of the cabins so that the wind could only bump her against the porch rails, not knock her down.

Grandma Tiley was startled, then grinned as Celia helped her wrestle open her door, then close it, wrenching it away from the pinning force of the wind.

"Leave Daniel with me," Grandma Tiley said as soon as they were safely inside. "I can carry him away. I ain't feeble, you know that. It'll rain 'fore that, anyway."

Celia smiled, admitting to herself that this was what she had wanted to hear, that it was what she had come for.

Grandma Tiley nodded. "You go an' help your man. Jus' make sure you both come home."

"Thank you," Celia said breathlessly, and she waited until the old woman had Daniel settled into the crib box. Then she struggled back out the door. Lightning cracked the sky wide open. Celia felt her mouth go dry with fear. But she shook her fist at the sky, ducked her head, and ran for the stables.

18

❧

Madelaine headed straight into the gale, looking
ahead of herself through slitted eyes. She had never
felt a wind like this, and it was both strange and oddly
thrilling. It seemed to reach inside her, raising a storm
of feelings inside her heart. It stole her breath, lifting
her almost off the ground.

The lightning was coming farther apart now, and
twice she had to stop, confused and unsure which way
to go in the darkness. Then the wind would ease
slightly, and she could open her eyes wide enough to
see the red glow of the fire through the trees.

It was hard to walk in the orchard. Limbs thrashed
and jerked, the twigs snagging at her dress. Her slippers barely protected her feet from the sharp ends of
the branches she stumbled through. Something
wrapped around her leg, and she jumped, startled,
then realized it was cloth, some kind of homespun
sack. She picked it up and hung on to it, using it to

shield her hands and forearms from the windborne bits of wood and dirt.

Stumbling, she caught her skirt, then tore it free. She longed to use the road but knew that anyone she passed would force her to go back to the house. The wind roared all around her, and every step was a shoving match, but the light of the fire drew closer every time Madelaine managed to look up, squinting against the rushing wind. Madelaine was scared, but she kept going. If she didn't, Françoise would never know that she loved him.

The sudden blow to her back and shoulder caught her off guard, and she stumbled, falling to the ground, lost in the sound of the wind and the pain that took her breath away. Then everything disappeared, even the sound of the wind.

Françoise waited for the next flash of lightning, scanning the road wildly when it came, but could not spot Quinn before the sky went black overhead. He faded a little farther back into the trees, watching the slaves line up. The line fell into place, and buckets full of water from the creek were passed along it from hand to hand, the last man in line turning to throw the water on the fire, then running toward the creek to refill the bucket he held, passing it up the line. Françoise moved farther away, crossing the creek upstream from the line, waiting for lightning to light the way.

The wind was getting stronger. It was a hurricane, no doubt about that now. His heart constricted at the idea of spending another hellish night in the open in a murderous wind. He was not sure he could survive it twice. And the deadly barrage of torn limbs had missed him by sheer good fortune last time. This time, his luck might not hold.

He came up onto the road above the fire fighters and waited for another overhead sparkle of lightning. This time, he saw Sheldon arriving, his horse no longer galloping but shambling head down and trembling as he forced it toward the fire. Behind him walked a ragged brigade of Cajuns. Monsieur LeBlanc was gesturing wildly at them, shouting, his voice lost on the wind. Françoise could not spot Philippe. There was no sign of Rory Quinn. Then the sky went black once more.

Françoise turned and headed away from the fire. One more man would make very little difference now. If the rain came, it would put out the fire. If not, there was going to be no stopping it. Françoise knew one thing for certain. If his house was burning, Monsieur LeBlanc and his friend Rory Quinn would do nothing to stop the fire.

Françoise turned his face out of the wind and started walking, bracing himself, leaning back against the force of the gale to keep from being knocked flat. They could fight their own damned fire. He was going to make sure that nothing happened to Madelaine.

When old Henry pointed, Gabriel turned to look. What he saw astonished him. Celia was coming up the bucket line, her face lit by the dancing flames. For a split second, he was furious with her. But before his rage could shape itself into words, the sky was illuminated by arcing white bolts of lightning. Gabriel took a step forward, ready to steady her, but she waved him off, her head high.

"Daniel is safe with Grandma Tiley," she shouted at him, then took a place in line in front of Henry.

As the storm roared, lightning splitting the sky, Gabriel was proud of his wife. She was strong, and she passed the heavy pails of water as well as any man, shouting encouragement to Henry and reaching out so that he wouldn't have to. Gabriel kept glancing at her, glad she was close. He turned so that their shoulders touched, then stood beside her against the howling wind.

Françoise only cut through the trees to avoid being seen. Walking through the orchards was suicidal, and he knew it. He stumbled through the fallen limbs, listening to the trees groan and strain in the wind. The lightning was less frequent now, but the bolts were brighter and lasted longer—long enough for him to be recognized. Wherever Quinn had gone, Françoise didn't want to run into him.

The next arcing display of blue-white light seemed to hang in the air. Squinting, Françoise saw something odd at the base of a peach tree up ahead. He veered away from it, then, listening to some inner counsel, veered back and headed toward it.

When lightning flashed again, he tried to memorize the image he saw, then to puzzle it out as he struggled toward it. It looked like a bag of laundry, spilled sideways and scattering in the wind. He was afraid it was someone hurt, or even dead.

When the next bolt of lightning came, it was bright but winked out before Françoise could do more than run forward a few steps, kicking aside a cottonade sack, then standing over the billowing flower-printed cloth. In the darkness, he knelt and reached out, his fear confirmed instantly. It was a woman's dress, and she lay where she had fallen, a heavy limb balanced across her back. He stood to pick it up, throwing the wood clear, then knelt again, wishing for lightning.

As if the heavens heard his thoughts, there was a dazzling crisscross of brilliant veins of blue-white light overhead. Françoise struggled with the blowing dress, pulling it away from the woman's face just in time to recognize Madelaine before the light winked out again.

Shaking, terrified of the bloodstain he had seen on the flowered fabric of her dress, he managed to pick her up and turn back out of the wind as he started for the house.

The wind pushed and shoved at him from behind, but he was steadier now than before, with Madelaine's weight added to his own. He could feel her slender waist in the circle of his right arm. Her feet swung as he walked, tapping against his leg. He angled his path to take him up out of the orchards and onto the road. The quicker she got help, the better, never mind who saw him or what happened after that.

As he labored forward, the wind howled past his ears, deafening him. A shard of something struck him in the back of his leg, and he very nearly fell, limping to ease the sudden pain. He squinted, trying to see in the darkness. To get back to the big house, he had to follow the road through the center of the orchard. One wind-hurtled limb could kill them both. And it was so far away. But the sugarhouse was farther, and the stables were too close to the line of the fire.

Françoise thought of the granary with its heavy-timbered walls, freshly plastered. It had stood through the last two hurricanes, and it was closer than any other shelter he knew about. He changed direction once more and prayed that God would protect them until he could carry Madelaine safely out of the trees. Then he prayed for lightning to show him the way. A few seconds later, it came, sparkling overhead long enough for him to see the hexagonal shape of the granary through the trees.

He headed toward it, resolute, refusing to feel the pain in his leg or the fear in his heart. To his astonishment, halfway there, he felt Madelaine's weight shift and looked down to see that she had opened her eyes. She went rigid, then relaxed again when she recognized him. After a few steps, he felt her reach up to put her arms around his neck, hiding her face from the wind. His heart rose. She was not gravely injured, then. If he could just get her to shelter, then back into her mother's care, she would be all right.

Rory was frantic to find the Cajun. It was imperative that no one else saw him, no one else knew he was at the fire *helping*. Who would start a fire, then stay to help put it out? The story was never going to hold if Françoise were spotted.

Rory had crossed the road almost at a run, then slowed when he had to duck beneath the cow pasture fence. When he stood up, there was a flash of lightning. He had looked anxiously at the end of the cow shed where the Cajun had been beating out the flames. The man was gone.

Cursing, Rory could only search, wishing he had armed himself. Maybe if he just beat the Cajun, put enough fear into him, the man would agree to disappear forever. And then, once things had died down, Rory would help the nightriders find him. Or maybe, Rory thought, he could pretend to strike a bargain, the Cajun's leaving for his own silence about the dalliance with Madelaine. He grinned as he scrambled beneath the opposite fence and found himself back in the orchard. Lightning flared above, and he looked around. Françoise was nowhere to be seen, but Rory stared at the writhing, twisting limbs of the trees and began to relax. If the Cajun had tried to cross the orchards, the storm might take care of him in its own way.

Rory glanced back at the fire. Monsieur LeBlanc was shouting at the slaves, his hands cupped around his mouth, urging them to fill the buckets faster. It was hard to see with the wind, tears streaming in his eyes, but he found Sheldon's distinctively pudgy silhouette obvious against the wall of flame.

From this distance, Rory could see what he hadn't realized up close. The flames on the buildings were whipped into a dancing frenzy, but fire wasn't spreading as fast as he had been afraid it might. The wind was so strong it blew unsheltered flames out without benefit of water.

Rory used the next flash of lightning to look around a second time. Maybe the Cajun had gone to hide near his *pirogue*, knowing that he had been seen. Perhaps he would wait for the weather to break, holed up somewhere, leaving at the first chance. That would settle matters nicely enough.

Rory almost smiled, turning, then he stopped. Françoise had seen him, so he had been able to see the others as well. He had seen Monsieur LeBlanc, Sheldon, Earley, and himself fighting the fire. That meant there were only women at the big house.

Cursing his own stupidity, Rory whirled around and ran toward the road, stumbling and falling twice before he gave in and slowed down. As he hurried toward the house, it began to rain, the first scattered drops like wind-driven bullets, bruising his face. As he trudged onward, the wind slowed a little and buffeted him at an angle. The storm was coming around. He could only hope the second half was no worse than the first.

When Madame LeBlanc heard the pounding on the door, she at first thought it was some trick of the wind. Then she heard a man's voice, loud and desperate. She got to her feet. Lily and Hope were huddled in their quarters, praying together. She reached for the door bar, then withdrew her hand. She was alone with only slave women to call if she needed help.

"Madelaine!" The single word came through the door, and her fingers flew back to the bar, wrenching it backward. She did not have to open the door; the wind flung it wide, knocking her backward, rushing in at a sharp angle that rattled the flour bins. A man staggered inside, blond hair showing from beneath his pulled-up jacket collar.

"Rory?" she said loudly, to be heard over the wind.

"Where's Madelaine?" he demanded, cutting her off as he turned back to wrestle the door closed again.

Madame LeBlanc glared at him. "She's upstairs, dawdling over dressing. I have not bothered her because I am sure she is frightened." She kept her voice even and calm, though her heart was pounding in fear and anger at his rudeness. "And my husband is all right?" she added coldly.

"Yes," Rory told her without a shred of apology in his manner. Then he took a deep breath and faced her, looking desperate and wild. "Please go upstairs and see if Madelaine is all right."

Madame LeBlanc forgave him his rudeness as she lit a lamp to carry. Of course. He loved the girl, and he was concerned for her safety, distracted by worry for her. She thought about calling Hope or Lily but decided not to. If either of them was weeping or frightened witless, she did not want Madelaine catching the vapors from them.

Madame LeBlanc swept through the kitchen door, crossing the carpeted expanse to the stairway. She went up with her head high and her spine straight, conscious that Rory had followed her and was watching from the foot of the stairs. She would give him a good example of calm, intelligent womanhood. And she hoped that Madelaine would do the same.

"Madelaine?" Madame LeBlanc eased her daughter's door open and went inside, frowning at the darkness in the room. "Madelaine?"

There was no answer.

Mistress LeBlanc called once more, then turned, surprised to hear Rory coming up the stairs, shouting her daughter's name. He flung open the door, and they stood, side by side, staring into the empty bedroom.

The granary door had blown off, but Françoise carried Madelaine inside anyway, ducking out of the sideways rain that was coming in scattered sheets.

Once inside, he straightened, feeling the stillness of the air like a kind touch. He found his way in the dark and finally stopped behind one of the plastered partition walls. He set Madelaine down slowly, carefully. Here in the darkness, there was an odd stillness that seemed unnatural after the incessant force of the wind outside. He could hear his own breathing and tried to quiet it.

Madelaine leaned against him. He held her gently, remembering the blood he had seen on her dress. "Are you badly hurt?"

She swayed a little on her feet, and he could tell she was stretching, seeing if she could stand on her own. She took in a quick breath, a soft sound of pain.

"What?" He leaned back, wishing desperately for a candle.

"I can't tell. But it hurts. Not too badly." Her voice was small and scared.

Françoise reached out to hold her again, and she rested

against him for a long moment. Then she stood on her own again, leaving one hand on his shoulder. "I was coming to give you a message. I wanted to tell you something."

He heard her, but for a few seconds the words made no sense. "To tell me . . ." he said, trailing off.

"That I love you." She said it with certainty.

"I want that to be true with all my heart," he told her, raising his voice against the rushing backdrop of the wind outside.

"It is true," she assured him. And in the dark, lifting her face to his, she kissed him in a way he had never presumed—or hoped—to kiss her. Then they both sank to the floor. She snuggled close, and they sat still, listening to the howling wind outside.

Celia flinched only a little with every flash of lightning. She took a bucket from Henry and handed it to Gabriel.

"I saw Françoise," he shouted close to her ear. "Here," he added, "fightin' this fire."

Celia looked at him, astonished. Why would Françoise have stayed? And if he stayed, why in the world would he have shown himself in order to help? A thin spatter of cold rain hit her face as she took the next bucket from Henry and turned, handing it off to Gabriel. She was shorter, and she had to lift it higher, even though he leaned toward her every time.

"Where'd he go?" Celia shouted at Gabriel.

He shrugged, answering close to her ear so that she could hear him. "He was down at the end shed when we got here, beatin' at the fire with his jacket."

Celia glanced the way Gabriel gestured, hoping that Françoise had found shelter somewhere and that he would get away safely when the hurricane passed. That was all she had time to think before Henry turned, a full bucket of water in his hands. The wind was still rising. It wouldn't be long before they all had to give up and seek shelter.

Another spatter of rain hit her cheeks, and she looked up, squinting. The spatters thickened, and she dared to hope. Moments later, the rain was a steady, wind-thrashed downpour.

A cheer broke out down the line, and people began making their way up the road back toward their cabins, none of them knowing or caring whether they had permission to leave. Gabriel took her hand, setting the last full bucket beside the road. They walked slowly, holding each other steady as the sheets of rain slammed at them.

19

Rory went through the house in a rage, shouting Madelaine's name. Madame LeBlanc was frantic, weeping and calling, supported by a tall, impassive servant woman. The cook had come out to see what the shouting was for but then had disappeared again after they had searched the whole house.

Rory banged open every door, ready to kill the Cajun if the man was dim-witted enough to be caught in the house. Finally, his anger still white-hot, he had to admit that Madelaine and her illicit lover were no longer in the house at all. *How dare that filthy Cajun mongrel come into this house?* Rory screamed inside his thoughts. *How dare he? For this, he will die.* There was no other response emphatic enough. If this went unpunished, no decent family in the parish was safe.

"Oh, please, find her," Madame LeBlanc was repeating over and over, coming down the hall toward him. She wobbled along, pale as milk, supported by the tall, somber servant who usually served dinner. "Where could she be, Hope?" Madame LeBlanc lamented. "Where could she possibly have gone?" The servant murmured some response, intended to soothe, but her mistress only wailed louder. "If she is out in this, this . . ." and she began to weep.

Rory longed to find Madelaine before the Cajun had time to spoil her purity. He would still marry her. She was very young, and this Cajun had obviously charmed and seduced her. She would outgrow her folly. But if the Cajun lived, or rumors began, Rory would reconsider. He wanted no shadow of scandal on his family life.

"I will do my best," Rory said aloud, nearly shouting.

Madame LeBlanc gasped and fell silent, wringing her hands. He made his way past her, saying something reassuring over his shoulder as he pounded down the stairs. He stopped only once, to get his pistol from his room. He tucked it beneath his jacket, then came out, and was halfway to the kitchen before Madame LeBlanc had time to mince her way down the stairs.

Instead of being hard to open, the kitchen door nearly leaped out of his hand this time. The wind had changed, and the rain had started. He started back toward the stables, trying to figure out where the Cajun would have gone to seek shelter. He had to be holed up somewhere—with Madelaine, most likely. He could not possibly be foolish enough to try to paddle a *pirogue* homeward in this raging storm.

* * *

Celia and Gabriel sat side by side in their cabin, holding hands. They had waited at Grandma Tiley's for the wind to drop a little as it shifted directions, then they had run, Gabriel carrying Daniel, back to their own place. Fighting the door closed, Celia had seen Master Sheldon riding toward his house out beyond the sheep pasture, his horse's head down, tail streaming out behind. It was time for everyone to get inside. The rain was coming in solid sliver-black sheets. The hurricane was not through with them yet.

Monsieur LeBlanc stood in the wind, knowing he should start home. The wind was shifting, but after a little lull, it was picking up speed, he could feel it. The tail end of the storm was going to be worse. Usually, it went the other way around, but not always. He knew why. It meant the storm was big, probably, with half the great circle of wind still out over the ocean.

He braced himself against a peach tree, resting for a moment, his clothes plastered to his skin by the relentless rain. He had told Sheldon to get the Cajuns to the sugarhouse for shelter, then to head home. Old Henry had decided to stay in his barn, alone, rather than go with his sons back to the cabins. The mares were in, and the fire was out, thanks to the short torrent of rain.

Monsieur LeBlanc started forward again, realizing that he could see the ground a little. He glanced upward. The sky was getting light along the horizon. The night had passed? The rain forced him to look down again, and he stumbled forward, using one, then another of the peach trunks to hold himself steady. They were jagged statues now, most of their limbs broken, littering the ground.

Monsieur LeBlanc's right foot hooked in a tangle of fallen limbs, and he pitched forward. A shooting pain wrenched upward from his ankle an instant before he hit the ground. He cried out, but the wind took his voice and scattered it into nothingness, muted by the pounding of the rain.

Crawling, realizing that he stood no chance at all of making it back to his house now, he thought desperately. The nearest shelter was the granary. Whether it would stand against this storm, he wasn't sure. But he thought he might be able to reach it, and that was as much as he could hope for now. He thought about his wife and daughter and was grateful both were safe and dry in the big house.

Fumbling at the branches, he picked up a straight branch longer than his arm and two inches thick. Using it as a cane, he forced himself to stand up and keep going.

Rory had struggled back toward the barn, but before he got close, he stopped, the rain hammering at him. He tried to guess what the Cajun would do now that he had Madelaine—if he did. It was possible that the scatterbrained girl had ventured out on her own, but he doubted it.

The one thing Rory was sure of was that the Cajun was still somewhere close. The man was not suicidal. He would not have taken his *pirogue* out onto the bayou in this weather, with or without Madelaine.

Rory thought about the sugarhouse. He had heard LeBlanc ordering Sheldon to get the Cajuns sheltered there. Maybe Françoise, hiding, would have fallen in with them? No, Rory thought, staggering forward as the wind shoved him along. The Cajun would be looking for a place that no one else would think of, *especially* if he had Madelaine with him.

Rory squinted into rain, realizing he could see the outlines of the trees and the roofline of the granary; dawn was close. He almost smiled as he angled across the driven rain, heading toward the building. The wind was still rising, and the rain was like driven pebbles now, bruising him. Tree limbs flailed in the dusky morning light, and torn-up, unrecognizable pieces of wind-pummeled debris hit his legs, then went on, rolling and leaping like live things.

Rory fought to keep moving. More than anything, he needed shelter. Maybe the Cajun wouldn't find any and would die exposed. If Madelaine were with him, that would be a terrible shame. If not, Rory would count it a blessing.

Madelaine had fallen asleep against Françoise's chest, but she wakened over and over, always to the sound of the wind. He stirred when she did, holding her closer, telling her they would be all right, that the hurricane would soon be gone. She believed him, exhausted beyond wondering what the morning would mean.

Waking this time, Madelaine heard the strength in the wind and felt the granary walls trembling beneath the sheer force of it. She sat up straighter, and Françoise moved a little to accommodate her shift, letting her know he was awake by tightening his arm around her shoulders after she had changed position.

Madelaine blinked, afraid. The storm sounded worse. A scraping sound drew her attention, and a second later, a sharp, blue-white light sparkled to life, dazzling her eyes.

"I thought so," a man's voice said. "Even though I hoped not."

Madelaine felt Françoise jerk upright. He tensed, and she felt him nudging her to one side. She moved, her eyes on Rory's face. He was not handsome now. He was sneering, his face distorted by hate. "You can't possibly think that you are going to get away with this."

"Françoise saved my life!" Madelaine said as steadily as she could.

Rory laughed as the match went out. "Really? But he's the one who talked you into risking it in the first place, isn't he?"

Madelaine got slowly to her feet as he struck another match, realizing what he must think. "I left the house of my own will."

She felt Françoise move another few inches away from her, his hand at the small of her back, gently keeping her where she was.

"Monsieur LeBlanc will end up leading the nightriders himself this time," Rory said, his voice laden with fury. "Between setting his barns on fire and kidnapping his daughter, I would say you have very little—"

"He didn't kidnap me," Madelaine said again, forcing her voice to stay even. "I came to find him. And I might have died in the orchard if he hadn't come across me lying there."

The sound of the wind was getting louder, and Madelaine heard the scraping noise on the floor on the other side of the partition wall. Rats, no doubt. She was too angry to shudder at the thought. "My father will believe me," she added, and Rory laughed again. Françoise was pushing her gently, and she moved another few inches away from him as unobtrusively as she could, uneasy, wishing he would put his arm around her and stand closer.

"I started no fires," Françoise said. Madelaine looked sidelong at him. She could see his face now. Early-morning light was coming in through the high windows.

Rory laughed. "I know that. But Monsieur LeBlanc won't."

Madelaine suddenly remembered Rory, his face dripping sweat, putting the lamp oil bottle back nearly empty. "You did it," she said, incredulous. "You set the fire!"

Rory backed up a step. He reached beneath his coat. An instant later, she saw a pistol in his hand.

"Let her go into the other room," Françoise said, and his voice was low and controlled.

Rory gestured with the pistol. "Go ahead. Stay clear of the door. And be quiet. This is between us."

"Why would you set the fire?" Madelaine demanded, furious with him. "It could have spread. You could have killed the horses in the barn, or even people if the quarter or the big house had caught fire."

Françoise gripped her arm. "Go now, Madelaine. He wants to hurt me, not you."

"I do, indeed," Rory said, raising his voice against the wind. "I set the fires thinking that I could get LeBlanc and the nightriders to do it for me, but I will have to do it myself, after all." He looked at Madelaine. "I will just say I found him attacking you after he dragged you from the safety of your home."

Madelaine felt Françoise's hand on her back again, nudging, pushing. She resisted the pressure. "My father will never believe that. I'll tell him—"

"And I will tell him about your Celia and her husband carrying messages. About how Celia stole lamp oil for him to start the fire. Your father will believe me. He will think this Cajun charmed you into thinking you love him."

"I do love him!" Madelaine shouted. But she knew Papa might believe Rory. The thought made all her anger, all her sorrow, rush together. She tried to speak and couldn't.

"You know I am right," Rory taunted her. "That's what's wrong with you—you can't accept the world you were born into." He paused. "Nothing to say to that?" Rory asked. He lifted the pistol, and he looked exhilarated, his face flushed in the early light. "It's right that this man pay with his life," Rory said reasonably. "No decent family in this parish wants to believe that men like him can take advantage of their daughters."

"He hasn't done anything wrong!" Madelaine shouted desperately, staring at the gun. "And you set the fire. My father will see through you, and he will—"

Rory waved the pistol, and she stopped, afraid of the fury on his face. "I set the fire intending to blame it on this low-born Cajun. As it turns out, he has helped me by staying when he should not have and by being foolish enough to be found with you."

"We did nothing wrong!" Madelaine screamed, even though she could feel Françoise's hand tighten on her arm. He was pushing her, an inch at a time, away from him.

"Be still!" Rory shouted at her.

Madelaine glanced at Françoise. He had not said a word and was still gently, relentlessly guiding her away from his side. He nodded, using his chin to indicate the direction she should go. "Please," he said, just loudly enough for her to hear. "Go to the other side of the wall. And stay down."

At that instant, Madelaine saw a quick movement in the shadows. A man came forward, lurching to one side, holding one arm high, then slashing downward. Rory cried out, then hunched over, holding his wrist and moaning. The pistol spun in a circle on the granary floor near her foot, and Madelaine stepped away from it. Françoise gathered her into his arms. It was only then that she recognized her father as he picked it up. He had a peach limb in his hand.

"Go into the other room," he told Rory, keeping the pistol pointed at the floor.

"You are crazy to protect this Cajun, sir. I will be only too glad to leave this place," Rory said, still gripping his wrist, his face contorted, his voice sharp and angry.

"Not as glad as I will be to see you go," Madelaine

heard her father growl over the sound of the wind. He watched Rory leave the room, then faced Madelaine. "I think we have a lot of talking to do, daughter," he said, and his voice was tight with pain.

"Are you hurt, Papa?" Madelaine stepped forward, and he put his arm around her shoulders to steady himself.

"Do you love him?" he asked, leaning close enough so that she felt his lips brush her ear.

"I do," Madelaine said. "He is a good man with a good heart." She leaned toward him. "He wants me to be a partner, a helpmeet. Can you understand? I cannot sit in the kitchen, waiting, as Maman does. I am not made to live as she does."

"He has nothing," her father countered.

"I don't care," Madelaine said, raising her voice and her head to look into his eyes. "Papa, I know you love me, but I don't care about hoops and embroidery and bankers' dinners. I don't. I want to *live*." She stared at him, willing him to believe what she was saying. Her heart was pounding inside her chest. She could hear her own fiery pulse above the roar of wind and rain. "I will run away if you forbid me to marry him."

"Madelaine!" Françoise chided her.

Lost in her own fury, Madelaine watched her father tilt his head. "You disapprove?"

Françoise nodded. "Of course. She should not lose her father's love because of me."

Madelaine braced her father as he lowered himself awkwardly to the floor. He grimaced and groaned. Françoise took off his jacket, laying it flat to cushion

Papa's swollen ankle. "Have you done anything improper to my daughter, sir?" Papa demanded once he was settled.

Françoise squatted to look him in the eye. "No. Nor would I ever harm her. I want to marry her."

"And I want to marry him, Papa," Madelaine said clearly, putting every bit of her resolve and determination into her voice. She stared at her father as he sat on the floor. It was odd to look down at him instead of up. He patted the ground beside him, gesturing for her to sit. "We probably have nothing to do but talk for a few hours at least," he said, his voice strained.

Françoise looked thoughtful, then lifted his chin. "Did you give it any thought? The peach trees, I mean?"

Madelaine stared, puzzled, as her father shook his head and smiled wryly. "A little." He sighed. "I think you're probably right. The trunk rot is made worse by pruning them that low."

Madelaine held her breath as Françoise answered and her father made another remark. Afraid to move or speak, she breathed silently and listened as they moved from peach trees to cane planting, then went on to talk about the indigo that had been grown in the region twenty years before.

Without making a sound, Madelaine sat slowly, then slid nearer Françoise. He put his arm around her and drew her close. As she listened to them talk farming, she began to feel safe for the first time in weeks. She closed her eyes, and their voices dimmed along with the morning light, and the ache of the bruise on her back, everything fading into the sound of the wind.

As the day got brighter, Françoise sat as still as he could, ignoring a cramp in his right leg, not wanting to waken Madelaine. He had the best news in the world for her, but it would wait while she slept. He could hear the voices from the other side of the partition wall, but he couldn't understand what the two men were saying. The wind was still high, but it was clearly dropping, and LeBlanc had wanted to settle matters and get Rory off his place as soon as possible.

Françoise still found the whole thing difficult to believe. Rory Quinn was an arrogant son of a wealthy man, though, and that made his view of the world very different from what any Cajun from the swamps could ever hope to understand. Somehow he had thought to get away with his ugly plan.

"What time is it?" Madelaine said in a sleepy voice.

"Almost nine by your father's watch half an hour or so ago. I'd say nine-thirty."

"Where is he?" she asked, as though she was just now remembering all that had happened. She sat up and flinched as her pain reminded her that she was hurt.

"Maman must be frantic."

Françoise nodded, smiling. "And she might not like your father giving us his permission to marry."

Madelaine sat up straight, her eyes going wide. He saw only happiness in them. "He did? Oh, Françoise!"

She embraced him, and Françoise held her tightly.

245

He had been watching her face very carefully. There had not been an instant of doubt, not a second's hesitation this time, either. He made a silent vow always to try to make her this happy. "There's more," he said close to her ear. "I asked him for a wedding present."

She pulled back, and her face changed, her eyes uncertain.

"I asked for the freedom of Celia, Gabriel, and their son."

Madelaine pressed her fingers to her lips. "What did he say?"

"He said it was an expensive gift but one he would be glad to give."

Madelaine smiled at him, and it was the smile of a woman in love. Françoise could not believe his good fortune. She was as lovely in her heart as in her face and form. "My father was a lucky man," he said aloud. "And so am I."

Glancing toward the gap in the partition wall to make sure her father was not in a position to see, Madelaine leaned close to be kissed.

About the Author

KATHLEEN DUEY loves research. Every morning she
walks from her bedroom to her office, steps through
the door and is transported backward in time. She
imagines wearing a hooped skirt that bounces with her
stride, the fabric trembling like a silk kite in the slight-
est breeze. She thinks about writing by candlelight,
the nib scratching across the paper, with ink-dark
shadows in the corners of the room deep enough to
hide someone watching. What would it be like to write
a friend a letter, then wait six months for an answer?
How could someone live in a house where you were
cold if you stepped a few feet away from the blazing
hearth? Imagine a life with no phone, no TV, no
schools, no sports, no streetlights, no cars, no com-
puters, no police, no firemen, no 911, no neighbors for
one or two—or fifty—miles.

Our lives are so different from our ancestors'. Yet the
circle of people's feelings and core concerns—love,
family, friendship, loyalty, ambition, recognition,
respect, achievement, envy, betrayal, fear, hatred, iso-
lation, loneliness—and back to love—has not changed
at all. *That's* the fascinating part of historical research

for Kathleen Duey. Everything has changed—and nothing has. Fashions, technology, customs and culture shift and reinvent themselves, but everyone still wants to be loved. They want to make it home safely and to sleep without listening for danger. Above all, everyone longs to find a kindred heart.